Round the World in Eighty Days

by

Jules Verne

Translated and simplified by
H. E. Palmer

Introduction and questions by
Richard Howat

Longman

Longman Group UK Limited
Longman House, Burnt Mill,
Harlow, Essex CM20 2JE, England
and Associated Companies throughout the world.

First published in the Longman Simplified English Series 1937
This edition first published in Longman Fiction 1993
Reprinted 1995

Set in 10.5/13pt Linotron 300 Expert Hass
Produced through Longman Malaysia, CL

ISBN 0 – 582 – 09671 5

The upper intermediate level books in the Longman Fiction series
are simplified to the 2,000 word level of the Longman Defining
Vocabulary, as researched for the *Longman Dictionary of Contemporary English*.

Contents

Introduction

If you mention Jules Verne's *Round the World in Eighty Days*, many people probably think of the film based on the book in which the British actor, David Niven, and the French comedian, Cantinflas, float away in a hot-air balloon. In fact, this incident was based, not on *Round the World in Eighty Days*, but on Jules Verne's first novel *Five Weeks in a Balloon*, which was published in 1862. *Round the World in Eighty Days* was published (in French) eleven years later and was an instant success. It was translated into several languages, but more extraordinarily, it inspired many attempts by people to copy and even outdo Phileas Fogg's remarkable journey.

For the author, Jules Verne, it was the high point in a career of many years as a struggling writer. He had been born in 1828 in Nantes, a port on the Atlantic coast of France. He studied law, but was more enthusiastic about becoming a writer. At first he wrote plays for the theatre in Paris, but had little success. He was interested in the sea, in travel and the transport revolution which changed the world so radically in the mid nineteenth century and these were the themes which he used as the background for *Round the World in Eighty Days*.

The steamship and the steam train were invented in the early nineteenth century. The first steamship crossed the Atlantic Ocean entirely under steam in 1833. Steam railways opened in England and the United States in about 1830. By the 1850s and 1860s, Europe and North America had a network of railways of thousands of miles, stretching across the entire continents. These developments affected Europe, America and the rest of the world. In America, steamships brought thousands of immigrants from Europe; the railways opened up the West and were also a strong unifying factor after the Civil War. The expanding British colonies could only be managed with a large navy of steamships and the building of railways across great stretches of the Middle East and in India.

At first, passengers, rather than freight, dominated the transport systems. Over 120 years later, when aeroplanes like Concorde can circle the world in hours, and spaceships can reach other planets in weeks, it is perhaps difficult for us to imagine the excitement of travelling great distances, to strange parts of the world, by train and steamship. But the speed and ease of the new forms of transport was thrilling nineteenth-century travellers.

There were plenty of uncertainties and surprises. For example, when the hero of *Round the World in Eighty Days*, Phileas Fogg, tries to cross India from Bombay to Calcutta, we discover that the railway is not yet complete, and so he must find some other way of continuing his journey — in this case on a rather expensive elephant. And when he and his manservant Passepartout reach North America, wanting to cross from the Pacific to the Atlantic coast, the journey is full of the dangers of the "Wild West": large herds of buffalo on the railroad, a broken bridge, and an attack by Indians.

Jules Verne did not only capture the excitement of this stage of technological progress. He also reflected a political "moment of history" — the extent of the British Empire at its peak. Two-thirds of Phileas Fogg's journey is through territory controlled by the British: Suez, India, Singapore and Hong Kong. Verne made this an important condition of the plot: as long as Fogg is in British territory, he is subject to British law and can be arrested as a suspected bank robber by the police detective, Mr Fix. This adds further tension to Fogg's race against the time limit which he has set himself.

Verne keeps the social and historical setting firmly in the background. The fun of the story is in the contrasting characters of the hero and his servant. Phileas Fogg represents a French view of the British Victorian gentleman — someone who is precise, cool and unemotional. He knows exactly how many steps it takes to walk from his home to the club. He knows exactly how many minutes it takes to get to the railway station. What is most extraordinary is his accurate prediction of how long it will take him to go round the world.

Passepartout, by contrast, is chaotic, unreliable and accident-prone — perhaps an Englishman's view of a Frenchman. He is the last kind of person you would expect to make a suitable travel companion for someone with a tight schedule. He is as much a threat to Fogg's plans to get round the world in eighty days as Mr Fix or the physical hazards of the journey.

And yet, by acts of luck and eccentric brilliance, Passepartout frequently saves the day. He finds the elephant which can take them sixty miles to the next railway. He saves the young Indian widow, Aouda, and he rescues the passengers who have been taken prisoner by the Sioux Indians. At the end, when Fogg thinks he has failed to reach his London club in time, it is Passepartout who discovers that all may not be lost and that Fogg may still win the bet. This setting of Passepartout's chaotic and impulsive nature against Phileas Fogg's precise and thoughtful one provides much of the humour and enjoyment of the story.

Another pleasure of the book is the wide range of colourful minor characters: Sir Francis Cromarty, the army officer; the Indian priests of Kali and the Calcutta judge; the various ships' captains whom Fogg hires and bribes to cross oceans at a minute's notice; William Batulcar, the circus manager in Yokohama and the noisy Yankee, Stamp W. Proctor in San Francisco. Jules Verne describes them all with humour and vitality. He has the ability of a great travel writer to show people both as representatives of different parts of the world, and as individuals with their own special peculiarities.

But it is the "race against time" which makes this book so attractive to such a wide range of readers, young and old, and in different cultures. The idea of racing is something which we all know about, whether we are children playing a board game, rally drivers crossing the roof of Africa, or the excited spectators of a marathon.

It was an idea of genius of Jules Verne to describe the most expansive race of all — a race around the world. It is a surprise race which starts only two hours after the idea is first raised. There is no equipment, no long training period, no complicated preparations. And the single competitor is also a surprise — a rather formal, non-sporting, English gentleman. Throughout the book, we constantly check Fogg's progress against his timetable: we worry about the delays and get excited about the way he solves problems. Sometimes we have great doubts about his ability to finish on time, but then, our confidence in him is restored. We want him to win, to do the "impossible", and secretly we know he will do it. The problems, setbacks and obstacles appear in order to tease us and test our confidence.

In this sense the story is a model of optimism, the great driving force of scientific and political development in the nineteenth century. It is no surprise that Jules Verne went on to become a politician supporting a range of political causes and fights for freedom. The challenge, the inventiveness and good humour of *Round the World in Eighty Days* can be a real inspiration for us all.

1

Mr Phileas Fogg and Passepartout

In the year 1872 there lived at No. 7 Savile Row, London, Mr Phileas Fogg, one of the members of the Reform Club. As he never spoke about himself, nobody knew who he was. He was certainly English, a fine-looking English gentleman. He was never seen at the bank or any place of business in the city. He was unknown to the world of shipowners and shipping. He was not a merchant or a business man. He was not a farmer. He was not a scientist. He was not a writer. He seemed to have no business or trade.

Phileas Fogg was a member of the Reform Club, and that was all.

As he seemed to be an unknown man, without friends, it may be wondered how he had come to be a member of the Reform Club. It was quite simple. The head of the bank that did his business had put his name on the list of those who wished to become members, and he was accepted.

Was Phileas Fogg rich? Yes, certainly. But how he had made his fortune nobody knew, and Mr Fogg was not the sort of man to tell anybody. He did not spend much money and yet he did not seem to be one of those people who loved saving money.

He talked very little; in fact nobody could have talked less. There was no secret about his habits and his daily life, but as he always did everything regularly in exactly the same way every day, people wondered more and more about him and his past life.

Had he travelled? Probably, for nobody knew the map of the world better than he. He seemed to have the most exact knowledge of every country and town in the world. Sometimes when the members of the club talked about travellers who had disappeared or become lost in some distant or unknown part of the world, Mr Fogg, in a few clear words, would explain what had probably become of them. His explanations often proved to be quite true. He was a man who must have travelled everywhere — at least in his mind and imagination.

It was quite certain, however, that for many years Phileas Fogg had not left London. Those who knew him a little better than others did, said that nobody had ever seen him in any other place than London. Even in London the only place where he was seen was the road between his house and the club. The only things he ever did were to read the newspapers and play cards. It was clear Mr Fogg did not play to win money, but for the sake of the game. For him a game of cards was a battle, a fight against a difficulty.

Phileas Fogg, it appeared, had neither a wife nor children — which may happen to the most honest people. Nobody had ever heard of his father or mother, or whether he had brothers and sisters. He lived alone in his house in Savile Row, where nobody ever paid him visits. Nothing was known about the inside of his house. One servant was enough to do the work. He had his meals at the club at exactly the same moments every day, when he sat in the same room, at the same table, always alone. He only went home to sleep, always exactly at midnight.

His home in Savile Row was a simple one, but very comfortable. His habits being so regular, and as he spent all the day at his club, his servant's duties were light. But Phileas Fogg expected from his servant an exceptional degree of exactness and regularity.

It was October 2nd. Mr Fogg had just told his servant, John Foster, that he would not need him any more. John Foster, had been guilty of a very serious irregularity: the hot water that he had brought to his master's room was only 84 degrees instead of 86 — and this mistake could not be excused. There was no pardon, and the servant must leave him. Mr Fogg was now waiting for his new servant, who was to appear between eleven o'clock and half past eleven.

Phileas Fogg was sitting in his armchair, his two feet together, his hands on his knees, his body straight and his head high. He was looking at the clock — a wonderful clock showing the seconds, the minutes, the hours, the days and the years. When half past eleven struck, Mr Fogg, according to his usual habit, would leave the house and go to the club.

At that moment there was a knock at the door. John Foster appeared.

"The new servant," he said.

A young man of about thirty years of age came in and bowed.

"You are a Frenchman and your name is John?" asked Mr Fogg.

"*Jean*, if you don't mind," answered the young man. "Jean Passepartout.* My name suits me very well because I am used to doing all sorts of things. I believe I am a good and honest fellow, but to tell you the truth, I have had many trades in my time. I have sung in the streets, I have been an acrobat and a dancer on a tightrope, and I have taught these subjects. In Paris I was an officer in the fire service, so that I can tell you stories of some of the most famous fires in that city. I left France five years ago. Wishing to know something of life in English homes, I came to England as a house-servant. Finding myself now without a situation I have come to you. I have heard that you, sir, lead the quietest and most regular life of any man in England. This will suit me very well for I, too, wish to lead a quiet life in the future, and even forget my name of *Passepartout*."

"You will suit me," answered Mr Fogg. "I have been told that you are a good servant and a man to be trusted. You know my conditions?"

"Yes, sir."

---

*'Passepartout': *a French word meaning* 'go anywhere' *or* 'fit anything'. *It is generally used as the name of a key that will fit any lock.*

"Very well. What is the time by your watch?"

"Twenty-two minutes past eleven," answered Passepartout pulling out of his pocket an immense silver watch.

"You are slow," said Mr Fogg.

"Excuse me, sir, but that is impossible."

"You are four minutes slow," said Mr Fogg. "But it does not matter so long as you know it. And now from this moment, eleven twenty-nine in the morning, Wednesday, October 2nd, 1872, you are in my service."

Having said this, Phileas Fogg stood up, took his hat with his left hand, put it on his head with a machine-like movement and left the house without another word.

After he had put his right foot before his left 575 times, and his left foot 576 times before his right, he reached the splendid building of the Reform Club. In the dining room there he took his usual place at the table. At twelve forty-seven he got up and went into the reading room, where one of the servants gave him a copy of *The Times* newspaper. He read this until three forty-five, when he took up the *Standard*, and read that until dinner. At five forty he was back again in the reading room, and gave his attention to the *Morning Chronicle*. Half an hour later he was joined by a few of his particular friends.

They began talking about a great bank robbery that had taken place the day before. The robber had stolen £55,000 in bank notes.

"The bank will lose its money, I think," said one of them, named Andrew Stuart.

"I don't think so," said another, named Thomas Flanagan. "The thief will be caught before long. As all the harbours are being carefully watched by the police, he will find it difficult to escape from the country."

"The *Morning Chronicle* thinks that the person who has taken the money is not an ordinary thief, but must be an educated man in some good position," said Mr Fogg.

They went on talking about the chances of the robber being caught or of the different ways he could escape from the country.

Some of the gentlemen said that the world was so large that a robber could easily get away from those who were trying to catch him. But Phileas Fogg did not agree with them.

"The world," he said, "is no longer a big place. Fast ships and trains have made a great change. For example," he went on, "we have now the Suez Canal, and railways now run across India and the United States."

Then they began to talk about how long it would take to go round the world. Most of them thought that three months would be needed, but Phileas Fogg said that eighty days would be enough.

To prove what he said, Mr Fogg took a piece of paper and wrote down:

London to Suez by Calais and Brindisi (railways and steamer)	7 days
Suez to Bombay (steamer)	13 "
Bombay to Calcutta (railway)	3 "
Calcutta to Hong Kong (steamer)	13 "
Hong Kong to Yokohama (steamer)	6 "
Yokohama to San Francisco (steamer)	22 "
San Francisco to New York (railway)	7 "
New York to London (steamer and railway)	9 "
	80 days

Mr Stuart said that it was impossible, and offered to bet four thousand pounds that he was right. Phileas Fogg said that he was ready to go round the world, himself, in eighty days; that he was ready to start that very evening. He said that he would not only agree to the bet of four thousand pounds with Mr Stuart, but that he would bet twenty thousand pounds of his fortune that he would go round the world in eighty days.

His five friends accepted the bet, and Mr Fogg warned them that they would have to pay for his journey.

"Now, that is agreed and arranged," said Mr Fogg. "I find that a train leaves for Dover at eight forty-five this evening. I shall travel by it."

"This very evening?" cried Mr Stuart, in a very surprised voice.

"This very evening," answered Fogg, as calmly as if it were a matter of going to the next street. "As this is Wednesday, October 2nd, I ought to be back in the reading room of the Reform Club on Saturday, December 21st, at eight forty-five in the evening, and if I am not, the twenty thousand pounds now in my bank will belong to you gentlemen."

Seven o'clock struck as he was speaking, and his friends advised him to hurry off at once and get ready for his journey. But he said there was no need for him to leave them just yet, as he was always ready; and so it was seven twenty-five before he said goodbye to his friends and left the club.

Twenty-five minutes later he opened the door of his house and found Passepartout waiting for him.

Passepartout was feeling very happy. He had been examining the house and the things in it, and had noticed its arrangements. Everything showed that his master was a man who lived a quiet and regular life. It was clear that he never went away on journeys, nor ever went hunting or shooting.

"This will suit me perfectly," he said to himself. "I have had many years of change and adventure, and I ask for nothing better than to lead a quiet and regular life with my new master. Splendid!"

Just then his master came in.

"We have to leave in ten minutes for Dover and Calais," said Phileas Fogg. "We are to go round the world in eighty days, so we must not lose any time."

The calmness with which he gave this information to his servant left that good Frenchman almost breathless with surprise.

"Round the world?"

"Yes, round the world."

"In eighty days?"

"In eighty days."

"Leaving in ten minutes' time?"

"Just so."

"But what about the things we are to take with us? What about packing?"

"We take nothing with us except our night-clothes. Everything else we shall buy on the way."

By eight o'clock Passepartout had done the few things that were to be done; he had packed a small travelling bag, and had locked up the rooms. Into the bag Mr Fogg put the big packet of bank notes, telling his servant to be careful of the bag, as there were twenty thousand pounds in it.

They locked the front door, and crossing the street, hired a carriage and drove quickly to Charing Cross Station. At the station were the five friends of Phileas Fogg to see him off, and he explained to them that he had a passport which he would get officials to sign at every important place on his journey, so as to prove that he had been there.

At eight forty-five the train began to move: the journey round the world had begun.

2

The Police-detective

Seven days later, while people were waiting at Suez for the steamer *Mongolia*, two men were having a serious talk. One was the British consul, and the other a thin, impatient little fellow whose eyes seemed never at rest. This man was Mr Fix, one of the many police-detectives sent out to the chief harbours to try to catch the bank robber of whom Mr Fogg and his friends had been talking.

Mr Fix had the idea that the robber might have chosen a new

way to go to America and, instead of crossing the Atlantic, might be going eastwards by way of India and Japan, and so escape being discovered.

The *Mongolia* was only to stop a short time at Suez and then go on to Bombay. As the passengers came off the boat they were all watched very carefully by the detective. One of those was Passepartout, who had been sent by his master to get the passport signed by the consul. He went up to Fix and, showing him the passport, explained that he wanted to find the consul. Fix took it and examined it closely. As he read on it the description of Mr Fogg, he became certain that it was the passport of the man he was trying to catch.

"This passport is not yours, is it?" he asked.

"No," said the other, "it belongs to my master."

"Where is your master?" asked Fix.

"On the ship," answered Passepartout.

"But he must go himself to the consul's office if he wants the passport to be signed by the consul. He cannot send anybody else in his place."

"Is that so?"

"Certainly."

"And where is the office?" asked Passepartout.

"Over there," said the detective, pointing.

"Then I will go and bring my master here," said Passepartout, "but he won't like having to come himself."

While Passepartout went back to the boat, the police-detective walked quickly to the consul's office, and told the consul what he thought.

"I am sure," he said, "that the man I am looking for is on board the *Mongolia.*"

"Very well, Mr Fix," answered the consul. "I shall not be sorry to see the fellow myself. But if he is, as you suppose, the robber, I don't think that he will come to my office. A thief does not like to show himself and talk about his business. Besides, passengers need not show their passports if they don't want to."

"But," said Fix, "he must not be allowed to go on to India. I must keep him here until I receive from London the warrant for his arrest."

"I can't help that," said the consul. If the man's passport is in order, I cannot stop him from going on to India."

At that moment two men came into the office. One was Passepartout and the other was Mr Fogg. Mr Fogg held out the passport and asked the consul to sign it.

The consul read it carefully, and then said:

"You are Mr Phileas Fogg?"

"I am."

"And this man is your servant?"

"Yes."

"You have come from London?"

"Yes."

"And you are going?"

" To Bombay."

"Very well, sir. You know that there is no need for you to bring this passport here for my signature."

"I know that," answered Mr Fogg, "but I wish to prove by your signature that I have passed through Suez."

"Very well," said the consul, and signed the passport.

A few minutes later Fix found Passepartout alone.

"Well, did you get what you wanted?"

"Oh, it's you, is it, sir? Yes, everything is all right. So this is Suez, and we are in Egypt."

"Just so."

"In Africa, I believe."

"Yes, in Africa."

"I wish I could stay longer, and see something of Africa. But we are travelling so quickly that there's no time for me to stop and see the interesting places."

"Are you in such a hurry, then?" asked Fix.

"No, but my master is. He is in a terrible hurry. We left London so suddenly that we had not even time to pack things for our journey."

"I can take you to a place where you can buy everything you

need," said Fix.

"You are really very kind," answered Passepartout.

As they walked along, the Frenchman said:

"Above all, I must not be too late for the boat!"

"You have plenty of time," answered Fix, "it's only twelve o'clock."

Passepartout pulled out his watch. "Twelve o'clock," said he. "You are joking. It is only eight minutes to ten."

"Your watch is slow," answered Fix.

"Slow? My watch? The watch that belonged to my father's grandfather? My watch that is never wrong? Impossible!"

"I see what it is," answered Fix. "You have kept London time, which is about two hours earlier than Suez time. You will have to put it right."

"Put it right!" cried Passepartout. "But it isn't wrong!"

"Well, if you don't, it will not agree with the sun."

"So much the worse for the sun, then, sir. The sun may be wrong, but not my watch."

A few minutes later, Fix said, "Let me see, you were saying that you left London in a hurry."

"We certainly did. On Wednesday evening Mr Fogg came back from his club much earlier than usual, and three-quarters of an hour after, we had started."

"But where is your master going?"

"He is going round the world."

"Going round the world?" cried Fix.

"Yes, in eighty days. A bet, he says it is, but between ourselves, I don't believe it. There's something about it that I don't understand."

"He seems to be a strange fellow."

"He certainly is."

"Is he rich?"

"He must be, and he is taking a lot of money with him, all in new bank notes. And he is spending his money, too, I can tell you."

"Have you known your master a long time?"

"I had never met him until the day we started. That was the day when I became his servant."

It is easy to imagine what result this talk had on the mind of the detective, who was already certain that Mr Fogg was the bank robber. This sudden journey in such a short time after the robbery; this anxiety to get to distant countries, under the excuse of a strange bet: all this made Fix feel quite sure that his idea was right. He made the Frenchman say more, and so learnt that the servant knew nothing of his master, that Mr Fogg lived alone in London, that he was known to be rich, that nobody knew where his fortune came from, that he was a man who never spoke about himself or his business. He found out, too, that he was really going on to Bombay.

"Is Bombay far?" asked Passepartout.

"Yes, rather," answered Fix. "It will take about another ten days of sailing."

"And where is Bombay?"

"In India."

"In Asia?"

"Of course."

Fix went to the consul a little after this talk. "I am now quite certain," he said, "that I have got him. He pretends to be trying to win a strange bet by going round the world in eighty days."

"Then he's very clever," said the consul. "He expects to get back safely to London after having escaped from the police all over the world."

"We shall see," answered Fix.

"You are sure that you are not mistaken?"

"Quite sure."

"Then why was he so anxious for me to sign his passport?"

"That's what I don't know, but listen." And then in a few words he told the consul what he had learnt from Passepartout.

"Yes, it really does seem," said the consul, "that he is the man you want. What are you going to do?"

"Send a telegram to London, telling the people there to send to me at Bombay an order for his arrest. Then I shall go on board the *Mongolia*, follow the thief to India, and there go up to him politely with the warrant in my hand and put my hand on his shoulder."

Then Fix said goodbye to the consul, sent the telegram, and went on board the *Mongolia*. Shortly after that the steamer was making its way through the Red Sea towards India.

Most of the passengers who had gone on board the *Mongolia* at Brindisi were not going farther than India. Some were going to Bombay; others to Calcutta, but by way of Bombay; for since a railway had been built that ran across the country from west to east, there was no need to make the long sea journey by way of Ceylon.

The day after the boat left Suez, Passepartout happened to see Fix.

"If I am not mistaken, sir," said he with a smile, "you are the one who so kindly directed me at Suez."

"Yes, of course, you are the servant of that strange Englishman."

"Just so, Mr . . ."

"Fix."

"Mr Fix, I am very pleased to find you on board. And where are you going?"

"Why, like you, to Bombay."

"That's splendid. Have you ever been there before?"

"Well . . . yes . . ." answered Fix, who did not want to say too much.

"Is India an interesting place?" asked Passepartout.

"Very interesting. There are all sorts of wonderful things to be seen there. I hope you will have plenty of time to see the country."

"I hope so too, Mr Fix. After all, it's a foolish thing to spend one's life jumping from a ship to a railway and from a railway to a ship, simply for the sake of going round the world in eighty days. No, all that sort of thing will come to an end at Bombay, I feel sure."

"And is Mr Fogg well?" asked Fix, without seeming to be very interested.

"Very well," answered Passepartout, "and so am I. I eat enough for three men. It's the sea air that makes me so hungry."

"I never see your master on the deck."

"No; he doesn't like mixing with other people."

"Do you know, Mr Passepartout, that this journey round the world in eighty days might be an excuse for something else, some secret purpose?"

"Well, Mr Fix, I don't know, and what is more, I don't want to know."

This talk was often followed by others, for the detective thought it wise to make friends with the servant of the man he was following: it might be useful.

At Aden, Fogg went on shore to have his passport signed. Passepartout went too, for he never lost a chance of seeing all that was to be seen.

"Very interesting," he said; "if one wants to see new things there is nothing so good as travelling."

On Sunday, October 20th, India came in sight.

3

The Train to Allahabad

The ship reached Bombay two days earlier than had been expected. At half past four in the evening the travellers went on shore, and the train for Calcutta was to leave at eight o'clock.

Mr Fogg, as you may imagine, went to the passport office; while Mr Fix went, as you may imagine, to the police station, where he asked anxiously whether the warrant had come.

It had not come. Fix was disappointed. He asked the chief of the Bombay police to give him an order to arrest Mr Fogg. The chief said no; it was a matter for the London police, and not his business at all. There was nothing to be done. He was fairly certain that Mr Fogg would go no farther than Bombay, and so he would wait until the order from London came, and he would then arrest him.

But by this time, Passepartout knew that the journey was not at an end. His master had told him that they would leave for Calcutta by the evening train, and so he began to think that, after all, the story of the bet was serious, and that they were really going round the world.

He went for a walk in the streets of Bombay, for he liked to see all there was to be seen. Unfortunately for him and his master, his wish to see everything resulted in serious trouble.

It was like this. While making his way towards the station he passed in front of the great temple of Malabar Hill. The outside of it looked so fine that he wanted to go and admire it from the inside, and he did so.

Now, there were two things that our sightseeing Frenchman did not know. One of them was this — that foreigners are not allowed to go inside Indian temples; the law was very severe on this point. The other was that even the Indians themselves were not allowed to go inside a temple with their shoes on; they must take off their shoes and leave them outside the door.

Passepartout went in, and he did not take his shoes off. While he was admiring the temple from the inside, three priests threw themselves upon him and pulled his shoes off and began giving him a good beating. Passepartout, strong and active, was easily able to get up, knock them down, fight his way out of the temple and run.

At five minutes to eight, only a few minutes before the train left, without any hat or shoes, he reached the railway station.

Fix was there. He had followed Mr Fogg and came to know that he was going to leave the town. He decided at once that he must follow him to Calcutta, and even farther. Passepartout did not see him, but Fix heard the explanations that he gave to his master and the story of his adventure.

"Don't let that happen again," said Phileas Fogg to his servant, as he took his place in the railway carriage.

Passepartout followed his master without saying anything more.

Fix was just going to get on the train himself when a better plan came into his mind.

"No, I will stay here," he said to himself. "The law has been broken here in India. I know what to do. I have got my man! "

Mr Fogg and Passepartout were not the only people in the railway carriage; there was a third traveller with them. This was Sir Francis Cromarty, an officer of the Indian Army, who was on his way to Benares.

On Tuesday morning, October 22nd, Sir Francis happened to ask Passepartout the time.

Passepartout pulled out his watch, looked at it, and answered, "Three o'clock."

"Impossible," said Sir Francis. "It must be seven o'clock at least."

"My watch is never wrong," replied Passepartout.

Sir Francis tried to make him understand that as they were going towards the east the days became shorter, and each degree that they passed made a difference of four minutes.

But Passepartout could not understand. His watch must be right, he said, and the sun must be wrong. His watch said that it was three o'clock and so it could not be seven o'clock.

As Sir Francis Cromarty became more and more friendly with his travelling companions, it was not long before he learnt what was the reason for their journey. He became most interested, and listened with the greatest care to what Mr Fogg told him. "You will be very fortunate, Mr Fogg," he said, "if you succeed in getting round the world in eighty days. All sorts of things may happen that will make you late. An accident; something unexpected ——"

"No," answered Mr Fogg, "even with accidents and un-expected happenings, I am certain to succeed."

"For example," answered Sir Francis, "this adventure of your servant at Bombay. You have no idea how severe the British government is in such matters. Your servant may be taken and punished ——"

"If my servant is caught and punished for going into a temple without taking his shoes off, it is his business and not mine. If he is stopped at Calcutta and put into prison, I shall, of course, be sorry. But it will not stop me from going on with my journey."

"But other things may happen that will make you late," answered Sir Francis.

At that moment the train came to a stop, and a voice was heard saying:

"All passengers get down here!"

Passepartout jumped out of the train to see what the matter was. In a few minutes he came back saying, "This is the end of the railway!"

"What do you mean?" asked Sir Francis.

"I mean that the train can go no farther."

The passengers got off the train.

"Where are we?" Sir Francis asked a railway official.

"We are at the village of Kholby."

"Why are we stopping?"

"This is where the railway line comes to an end."

"How's that?"

"It is not yet completed. The fifty miles of line between here and Allahabad has not yet been built."

"But the newspapers say that the line is complete."

"I can't help that," answered the official. "The newspapers have made a mistake."

"But we have paid for the journey from Bombay to Calcutta!" said Sir Francis.

"But the travellers know that they must find some way of their own to get from here to Allahabad."

Sir Francis was very angry. Passepartout was ready to fight

the railway official; he did not dare look at his master.

"Sir Francis," said Mr Fogg calmly, "we had better find another way of getting to Allahabad."

"Mr Fogg, this is going to put an end to your plan."

"Not at all, Sir Francis. I had expected it."

"What! You knew that the railway was not yet complete?"

"No, but I knew something or other of this sort was certain to happen. But this is not serious. I am two days early. There is a ship that leaves Calcutta for Hong Kong at twelve o'clock on the 25th; this is only the 22nd, and we shall get to Calcutta in time."

It was only too true that the railway ended at this point. The newspapers were mistaken — as they often are. Most of the passengers had known that the line stopped there, and had already hired carts, carriages and horses. So when Mr Fogg and Sir Francis went to find some way of getting to Allahabad everything had been taken.

"I shall walk," said Phileas Fogg.

But Passepartout had been more fortunate, and said, "I think I have found a way."

"And what's that?"

"An elephant. An elephant that belongs to an Indian who lives close by."

"Let's go and see the elephant," said Mr Fogg.

Five minutes later the three travellers reached a hut, inside of which was an Indian and outside of which was an elephant.

Mr Fogg asked if he could hire the animal. The Indian said no.

Fogg asked him again and offered the very high price of ten pounds an hour. The answer was no. Twenty pounds? No. Forty pounds? No.

Passepartout gave a jump every time the price went up.

It was a good price, all the same. If it took fifteen hours to get to Allahabad, the Indian would receive six hundred pounds.

Phileas Fogg, without showing any signs of impatience, offered to buy the elephant, and suggested a thousand pounds as the price.

The Indian did not want to sell.

Sir Francis Cromarty took Mr Fogg on one side and advised him to think the matter over before going any further.

Mr Fogg said that he never thought things over; he always decided things at once. He had to win a bet of twenty thousand pounds, and to win it, he must have the elephant, even if he paid twenty times the value of the animal.

Mr Fogg went back to the Indian. It was easy to see by the look on the man's face that the whole thing was a question of money. Phileas Fogg offered twelve hundred pounds, then fifteen hundred, then eighteen hundred, and at last two thousand pounds.

Then the Indian said he would sell.

The next thing was to find a man to drive it. This was easier. A young Indian, with a pleasant-looking face, offered his services. Mr Fogg promised him a good reward, which made his face look more pleased still. The Indian knew his business. He fitted on the animal a seating arrangement, with a chair on each side.

Mr Fogg paid the Indian in bank notes which he took from the bag. This made Passepartout feel almost ill. Then Mr Fogg offered to take Sir Francis Cromarty with him to Allahabad. Sir Francis accepted. One more traveller would not make the immense animal tired.

Food was bought in the village. Sir Francis took his place on one of the chairs, and Phileas Fogg on the other. The Indian took his place on the neck of the elephant, and Passepartout on its back.

At nine o'clock they started, and leaving the village took the path that ran through the forest.

They travelled all through the day, and by eight o'clock in the evening they had already got halfway to Allahabad. They started off at six o'clock the next morning, and the driver said that they would reach Allahabad that evening.

At about four o'clock in the afternoon, when they were in the middle of a thick forest, strange noises were suddenly heard, the noise of many voices crying, and the noise of wild music. What was it? The driver stopped; his face showed his anxiety; he jumped down, tied the elephant to a tree, and then crawled into the forest. A few moments later he came back, saying, "We must not be seen! Let us hide; there is danger." He untied the elephant, and led it to a place from which the travellers could not be seen.

The noises came nearer and nearer. The travellers watched, not knowing what they were going to see. Then there came in sight a crowd of priests half-walking and half-dancing, half-shouting and half-singing. Others came behind them pulling a sort of cart, or carriage. On this was sitting something in the shape of an immense man or woman with four arms, painted in violent colours.

Sir Francis knew what it was. "It is the Goddess Kali, the Goddess of Love and Death," he said.

"The Goddess of Death, perhaps," said Passepartout, "but the Goddess of Love, that I can never believe. What an ugly woman!"

The Indian made a sign to him to keep quiet.

Behind this some priests were pulling along a woman, who seemed hardly able to walk. She was young, and very beautiful.

Then came another group of priests carrying a dead body. The body was dressed in the fine clothes of an Indian prince.

4

A Suttee

Sir Francis looked at all this very sadly, and turning towards the Indian, said, "A *suttee*?"

The Indian answered yes.

When the priests had all passed, and their cries could be heard no longer, Mr Fogg turned to Sir Francis and asked him the meaning of the word *suttee*.

"A *suttee*," he answered, "is an offering to the gods of the body of a woman whose husband has died. This poor woman will be burnt tomorrow morning when the sun rises."

"Oh! the wicked people!" cried Passepartout.

"And the dead body?"

"The dead body is that of her husband, the prince," answered the driver.

"In most of India," explained Sir Francis Cromarty, "this sort of thing has been stopped. But we can do nothing in the case of the wilder parts of the country."

"The poor girl!" cried Passepartout, "to be burnt alive!"

"Yes," said Sir Francis, "burnt alive, and if she were not, you would hardly believe what cruelties she would suffer. They would cut off her hair, they would give her almost nothing to eat, people would treat her worse than a dog. So many of these unfortunate women prefer to be burnt than to lead such a terrible life. But there are cases in which the woman offers herself freely. I remember one such case when a young woman asked to be burnt with the body of her husband. The governor of course would not allow it. So the woman left the town and went into the country of one of the Indian princes, and there was able to die in the way she wished."

The driver, who had been listening, said, "The woman we saw

just now is not going to her death willingly; she is being forced."

"But," said Sir Francis, "she does not seem to be making any efforts to escape."

The Indian answered, "They have made her drink or smoke something that has put her into a sort of sleep. She does not know what is happening."

"But how do you know," asked Sir Francis, "that she is not going willingly?"

"Everybody round here knows the story," answered the man. "She is a girl of great beauty, the daughter of a rich merchant of Bombay. Her name is Aouda. Her father and mother died when she was young, and she was forced to marry this old prince. Three months later he died. Knowing what would happen to her, she escaped, and was caught shortly after. The brother of the prince would get the prince's fortune if this girl died, and so he has arranged for her to be put to death."

"Where are they taking her?" asked Mr Fogg.

"To the Pillaji temple, two miles from here. She will pass the night there waiting for the moment when she is to be burnt."

Just as they were going to start on their journey again, Mr Fogg turned to Sir Francis and said:

"Let us save this woman."

"Save this woman, Mr Fogg?" cried Sir Francis.

"I am still twelve hours early," he answered, "and I can give those twelve hours to her."

"Mr Fogg, you have a very kind heart!"

"Sometimes — when I have time," answered Mr Fogg, simply.

They decided to go as near to the temple as possible.

Half an hour later they came to a stop among some thick trees from where they could not be seen.

Then they talked as to the best plan for saving the girl. The Indian knew this temple, and said that the girl was inside it. Would it be possible to go in and take her away while the priests were asleep? Would it be possible to make a hole in the wall? Such things could not be decided until the right moment. But this much was certain, that if she was to be carried off, she must be carried off during the night, and not at the moment when she was being taken to the place of her death, for then no man could save her.

Mr Fogg and his companions waited for the night to come. When it got dark, at about six o'clock, they decided to go as far as the temple to see what could be done. By that time, no more noise was heard. The Indians had been drinking or smoking something that put them into a deep sleep; it would perhaps be possible to go into the temple without being noticed.

The Indian went first, and the others followed. Before long they came to the edge of a stream, and there they saw in front of them a pile of wood which had been built up by the Indians. On this pile of wood lay the body of the prince which was to be burnt at the same time as the girl whom they were trying to save. A few hundred feet on the other side of this was the temple.

"Follow me," said the driver, in a low voice.

A short time after, they came to a place where the ground was covered with the sleeping Indians. But to their disappointment, they saw men who were not asleep. They were walking up and down in front of the doors of the temple, on the watch. The travellers supposed that there must be men on the watch inside, too.

The Indian went no farther. He saw the impossibility of getting into the temple by its doors, and he went back to his companions.

Phileas Fogg and Sir Francis Cromarty understood as well as he did, that nothing was to be done on that side.

They talked over the matter in low voices.

"Let us wait," said Sir Francis. "It is only eight o'clock, and perhaps these men will go to sleep too, later."

"Perhaps they will," said Passepartout.

So Phileas Fogg and his companions lay down at the foot of a tree, and waited.

The time seemed very long. The Indian sometimes left them to watch what was happening.

At midnight the priests were still on the watch. It was clear that they did not mean to sleep. There was only one thing to be done, and that was to make a hole in the wall of the temple. But the question was: would the men inside the temple be on the watch in the same way as those outside?

After a last talk, the Indian said that he was ready to start. The others followed him.

Half an hour later they reached the back of the temple without having met anyone. There was no watch on this side, where there were neither doors nor windows.

It was a dark night. The moon was low down in the sky and almost covered with clouds. The thick trees made the darkness greater.

But it was one thing to get to the wall of the temple, and another to get inside it. To do this, Phileas Fogg and his companions had nothing except their pocket-knives. Fortunately the wall was made chiefly of wood.

They went to work, making as little noise as possible. The Indian and Passepartout made an opening. Suddenly a cry was heard from inside the temple, and at the same time another cry was heard from outside.

The workers stopped. What had happened? Had their work been heard? They went back to their hiding place among the trees and waited. Some time passed. Then they went back to the wall of the temple, looked through the hole that they had made, and saw that there were men inside who were on the watch round the place where the young girl was sleeping.

5

The Rescue of Aouda

It is difficult to describe the disappointment of the four men. They had got so near to the woman that they wished to save, but they could not save her. They had failed in their efforts. Sir Francis was biting his fingers. Passepartout was in a state of terrible anger. The Indian could not hide his feelings. Fogg showed no feeling at all; he was as calm as ever.

"The only thing that we can do is to go away," said Sir Francis, in a low voice.

"We must go away: that is all that we can do," said the Indian.

Passepartout said nothing.

"Let us wait," said Phileas Fogg. "I need not get to Allahabad before midday to-morrow."

"But what are you hoping for?" asked Sir Francis. "In a few hours daylight will come and then ——"

"The chance that we are hoping for may come at the last moment," answered Fogg.

Sir Francis wondered what Fogg was thinking. What was this cold Englishman depending upon? Was he going to throw himself upon the young woman and carry her off at the moment that the Indians were going to burn her?

To try to do that would be the act of a madman. But Phileas Fogg was not a madman. So Sir Francis decided to wait until the end.

The faithful Indian would not let his companions stay in the dangerous place in which they were, but made them come back to the safer place among the trees from where they could see everything but not be seen themselves.

But Passepartout, sitting on the lowest branches of a tree, had an idea, and he began to make a plan. At first he thought, "What a foolish plan! It cannot succeed." But later he thought, "Why not after all? It's a chance, perhaps the only one!" So then he began to crawl out on the low branches of the tree, the ends of which bent down towards the ground.

The hours went by, and at last there were signs that the sun would soon rise.

The moment had come. The sleeping men woke up; the singing and crying started again. The poor girl was now going to die.

The temple doors opened. Mr Fogg and Sir Francis Cromarty could see her as two priests carried her out. For one moment it looked as if she were going to make an effort to escape, but a moment later she fell back into the state of sleep caused by the stuff that they had made her smoke. The crowd of Indians went forward towards the pile of wood. Phileas Fogg and his companions followed. Two minutes later they reached the little stream, not fifty steps away from the pile on which the dead body of the prince lay. They could see the young woman lying beside him.

Oil had been thrown on the wood to make it burn easily. The priests brought fire, and a moment later the wood began to burn.

At that moment Sir Francis and the elephant driver held back Mr Fogg, who wanted to jump forward towards the fire. He threw them off . . . and a cry of terror was heard. All the Indians threw themselves on the ground in a state of fear.

The old prince, then, was not dead, after all. He was seen to stand up suddenly, to pick up the young woman in his arms and to come down from the pile of wood carrying her, among the clouds of smoke.

The priests and others turned their faces to the ground: they did not dare to look at the terrible sight. Mr Fogg and Sir Francis were in a state of the greatest surprise. The Indian bowed his head, and Passepartout must have been in a state of equal surprise.

The man who had come to life again, carrying the girl in his arms, came quickly towards the travellers, came up to them and said, "Let's go!"

It was Passepartout himself! During the night he had slipped off the branch and, unnoticed by the Indians, had climbed on the pile. There in the darkness he had put on the long golden coat which he took from the dead body of the prince, and lay down beside the body. In this way, when the right moment came, he was able to do what has just been described.

Acting with the greatest daring, he was fortunate enough to succeed. A moment later the four men disappeared into the wood, the elephant carrying them away as fast as it could go.

But the cries and shouts showed them that the trick had been discovered. For on the burning wood the real body of the old prince was clearly seen. The priests, having come back to their senses, came to understand that the young woman had been carried off. They tried to follow and catch the travellers, but they were too late.

An hour later Passepartout was still laughing over the success. Sir Francis had taken the brave fellow by the hand. His master had said, "Good", which, from him, meant very high praise. Passepartout answered that all the honour belonged to his master. He could only see the funny part of the business, and laughed to think that for a short time he had been the dead husband of a charming woman: an old Indian prince!

As for the girl, she had no idea of what had happened. She was still asleep.

The elephant moved quickly through the forest. An hour after leaving the temple the travellers came to a stretch of flat country. At seven o'clock they stopped to rest. The young woman was still in the same state. Sir Francis had no anxiety about her condition; he knew that in a few hours she would come to her senses and be all right. What he was afraid of was her future. He told Mr Fogg that if Aouda stayed in India, she would certainly, in the end, be caught again by those who wanted to kill her. She could be safe only when she was out of the country.

Phileas Fogg answered that he would think over the matter.

At ten o'clock they reached Allahabad. From this point the

railway started again, and trains ran in less than twenty-four hours from here to Calcutta.

Phileas Fogg should, then, get to Calcutta in time to take the boat that left there the next day, October 25th, at midday, for Hong Kong.

Mr Fogg found a room at the station for the young woman to rest in, and sent Passepartout to buy the clothes and other things that she would need.

By the time he got back to the station, Aouda was already much better. She was now awake, and understood, more or less, what had happened.

She was certainly beautiful. She spoke English perfectly, and was in every way a charming and educated woman.

6

Stopped by the Police

The train was just going to leave Allahabad Station. The Indian driver was waiting. Mr Fogg gave him the money he had promised, and no more. That rather surprised Passepartout, who knew how faithful the man had been. In fact, if the priests of the Pillaji temple later came to hear how he had helped in carrying off the woman that they were going to burn, they would never forgive him, and his life would be in danger.

Then there was the question of the elephant. What was to be done with this animal that had been bought at such a high price?

But Phileas Fogg had already come to a decision. He turned to the Indian and said:

"You have been useful and faithful. I have paid you for your service but not for your faithfulness and friendliness. Do you want this elephant? If so, it is yours."

"You are giving me a fortune!" he cried in answer.

"Take it, my good man, and even then I shall feel that I owe you something."

"Splendid!" cried Passepartout. "Take it, my friend. It is your reward!"

A few minutes later, Phileas Fogg, Sir Francis Cromarty and Passepartout, together with Aouda, were in a comfortable railway carriage making their way towards Benares. This town was eighty miles away from Allahabad, but they reached it in two hours.

During this journey the young woman came completely to herself. It may be better imagined than described how surprised she was to find herself dressed in European clothes, in a comfortable railway carriage, among companions who were quite strangers to her! Sir Francis Cromarty told her the story of how she had been saved. He spoke of the great kindness of Phileas Fogg, who had put his life in danger to save her, and of how the daring plan of Passepartout had succeeded.

In answer to these praises Mr Fogg said nothing, and Passepartout said simply, "Oh, it's not worth talking about!"

Aouda thanked those who had saved her, more by her tears than by her words: her eyes said more than her mouth. Then she began to think of the terrible time through which she had passed, and of the danger to her of living in India. She was frightened.

Phileas Fogg understood what she was thinking, and to put her mind at ease, and comfort her, told her — but very coldly — that he was going to take her to Hong Kong, where she could stay until everything had been forgotten.

Aouda was very grateful. It so happened that one of her uncles lived there — one of the chief merchants of this town on a small British island close to the coast of China.

At half past twelve the train stopped at Benares. Here Sir Francis Cromarty left them, after wishing them all success in their journey. "My hope is," he said, "that you will reach London in time to win your bet."

Aouda said that she would never forget how much he had helped in saving her from a terrible death.

Passepartout shook hands with him with such force that Sir Francis almost cried out with pain.

Mr Fogg touched his hand lightly, and said, "Thank you."

The train went on towards Calcutta, and reached there the next morning at seven o'clock. The boat did not leave until midday, and so Mr Fogg was five hours early.

As Mr Fogg was leaving the station, a policeman came up to him and said:

"Mr Phileas Fogg?"

"Yes," he answered, "that is my name."

"Is this man your servant?" asked the policeman.

"Yes."

"Please follow me, both of you."

Mr Fogg made no movement of surprise. The policeman was an officer of the law, and for every Englishman the law is something to be obeyed. Passepartout, being a Frenchman, said, "What do you want? What does this mean? Tell me this first." But the policeman touched him on the shoulder, and Phileas Fogg told him to obey.

"May this young lady come with us?" asked Mr Fogg.

"She may," answered the policeman.

The policeman took them towards a four-wheeled carriage with two horses. They got in and drove off. Nobody spoke during the journey, which lasted about twenty minutes.

At the police station they were taken into a room and told that they would be brought before the judge at half past eight. The policeman then left them, locking the door behind him.

"Well, we're caught!" cried Passepartout.

Aouda turned to Mr Fogg, saying, "You must leave me! It is because of me that the police have taken you! It is because you saved me!"

Fogg answered simply that that was not possible. To be brought before the judge for having saved a woman from those who were going to burn her? Impossible. There must be a mistake. Mr Fogg added that in any case he would not leave Aouda behind, and that he would take her with him to Hong Kong.

"But the boat leaves at twelve o'clock!" said Passepartout.

"Before twelve o'clock we shall be on board the boat," answered Mr Fogg.

He said it so seriously and naturally that Passepartout could not help saying to himself, "Yes, of course, that is certain. Before twelve o'clock we shall be on board."

At half past eight the door was opened. The policeman came and then took the prisoners to the hall.

The judge appeared a few moments later, and sat down.

"Call the first case," he said.

"Phileas Fogg!" called out an officer.

"I am here," answered Fogg.

"Passepartout!"

"I am here!" answered Passepartout.

"Very well," said the judge. "For the last two days we have been watching the trains from Bombay."

"But why?" asked Passepartout. "What have we done?"

"You will see," said the judge. "Call the complainants."

The door was opened, and three Indian priests came into the hall.

"That's what it is!" said Passepartout to himself. "Those are the fellows who were going to burn our young lady!"

The priests stood before the judge, while the official read out the complaint — that Phileas Fogg and his servant had broken the law by behaving in a violent and disorderly way while on the ground forming part of a temple.

"You have heard the complaint?" asked the judge.

"I have," answered Mr Fogg, looking at his watch.

"Is it true?"

"Yes, it is true, and I am waiting to hear those priests tell you what they were going to do at the Pillaji temple when we stopped them."

The priests looked at each other in surprise. They seemed not to understand what Fogg had said.

"Yes!" cried Passepartout impatiently, "at the temple of Pillaji, where they were going to burn the poor girl!"

The priests looked more and more surprised, and the judge could understand nothing.

"Burn whom?" asked the judge. "Whom were they going to burn in the middle of the town of Bombay?"

"Bombay?" cried Passepartout.

"Yes, of course. We know nothing about the temple of Pillaji; we are talking of the temple of Malabar Hill, in Bombay."

"And in proof," added the official, "here are the shoes." And he held up the shoes.

"My shoes!" cried Passepartout.

Phileas Fogg and his servant had quite forgotten what had happened at the temple in Bombay, but it was this that was the cause of their being brought before the judge in Calcutta.

Fix had seen at once how he could make use of the business of the shoes. He had been to the Bombay temple and had advised the priests to make a complaint to the government. If they did this, the man who had gone into the temple with his shoes on, and then knocked down the priests, would be forced to pay them a large sum of money. The priests agreed, and came with Fix to Calcutta by the next train.

Because of the time spent by Fogg and his companion in saving the young girl, Fix and the priests reached Calcutta first. Fix had sent a telegram from Bombay to the Calcutta police, telling them to stop Mr Fogg and Passepartout when they got off the train, so he was very disappointed when he learnt that nothing had been seen of them. He then thought that they had got off at one of the stations and were making their way towards the south of India. For twenty-four hours, suffering from terrible anxiety, he had been watching at the station. That morning his patience was rewarded when he saw the two men get off the train. He at once ordered a policeman to stop them and bring them before the judge. But who the woman was, and how she had come to join the other two, was more than he could understand.

If Passepartout had been paying less attention to his own business, he would have seen, sitting in a corner, Mr Fix, listening with the greatest interest to everything that was said. For at Calcutta, as at Bombay and Suez, the order of arrest had not yet reached him.

The judge noted that Passepartout had said that the shoes were his.

"You agree, then," said he, "that what has been said is true. You were inside the temple without taking off your shoes."

"Yes," said Passepartout.

"According to the English law," the judge went on, "the ideas of the Indians in such matters must be respected. It has been proved, and you agree, that you behaved in a disrespectful and disorderly way in the temple on Malabar Hill, Bombay, on October 20th. For this you will be kept in prison for fourteen days, and must pay three hundred pounds."

"Three hundred pounds?" cried Passepartout.

"And," added the judge, "although it has not been proved that Phileas Fogg had anything to do with the matter, he is the master of this man, and so must suffer for the fault of his servant. You will be kept in prison for seven days and pay a hundred and fifty pounds."

Fix, in his corner, was very happy. The order of arrest would certainly come before the seven days had passed.

Passepartout was in a terrible state, as may be imagined. His master's plans had failed; the bet would be lost, and Mr Fogg's whole fortune. And all because, like a fool, he had gone into that temple.

Mr Fogg showed no sign of disappointment. He said, calmly, "I offer bail."

"You have the right," said the judge.

This did not suit Mr Fix at all, but he felt no anxiety when he heard the judge say, "As Phileas Fogg and his servant are strangers, the amount of bail will be one thousand pounds for each."

"I will pay it," said Mr Fogg. And out of the bag that Passepartout was carrying he took a packet of bank notes and put them on the table of the official!

"This money will be given back to you when you come out of prison," said the judge.

"Come along," said Phileas Fogg to his servant.

"But at least they must give me back my shoes!" cried Passepartout, in an angry voice.

They gave him his shoes.

"They have cost a lot of money," he said. "More than a thousand pounds each! And they do not fit very well, either."

Passepartout, in a very unhappy state of mind, followed Mr Fogg, who had offered his arm to Aouda. Fix still hoped that the robber (as he thought Mr Fogg to be) would never agree to lose the two thousand pounds, and that he would go to prison for seven days. All the same, he followed him closely.

Mr Fogg took a carriage, and Aouda, Passepartout and he took their places in it.

Fix ran behind, and before long reached the harbour, where the carriage stopped.

Half a mile out at sea was the steamer *Rangoon*. It was eleven o'clock, and Mr Fogg was one hour early.

Fix saw him get down from the carriage and, with his companions, take his place in a boat, which at once started off in the direction of the *Rangoon*. The detective was violently angry.

"He has gone!" he cried, "and two thousand pounds have gone too! The robber! The thief! I will follow him to the end of the world, but at the rate he is spending the money, there will be nothing left of what he has stolen!"

The detective was right. As a matter of fact, since he had left London Mr Fogg had spent more than five thousand pounds — and as the money grew less, the less would be the reward of the detective.

7

Calcutta to Hong Kong

The *Rangoon* was a fine iron steamship, as fast as the *Mongolia* but not so comfortable. But, after all, it was only three thousand five hundred miles from Calcutta to Hong Kong — which meant eleven or twelve days only.

Aouda came to know Phileas Fogg much better, and told him how grateful she was to him for having saved her and for taking so much care of her. Mr Fogg listened to her in a very cold and distant way — at least it seemed so — and showed no sign of any friendly feelings towards her. He treated her, of course, with the greatest politeness, but it was the politeness of a machine. He took care that she had everything she needed for her comfort and came regularly to see her. If he did not talk much, he at least listened to her. Aouda found it difficult to understand his behaviour, but Passepartout explained to her something of his master's ways and habits. He told her, too, the reason for his journey round the world.

Aouda told Mr Fogg the story of her life, and spoke about her uncles, who were rich merchants, one in Bombay, and the other — whom she was going to join — at Hong Kong.

The weather was fine and the sea was calm, and the steamer made its way across the Bay of Bengal in the direction of Singapore.

The day before the *Rangoon* reached Singapore, Passepartout suddenly found himself face to face with Mr Fix.

"Why! Mr Fix! What are you doing here? I thought you were at Bombay? Are you travelling round the world too?"

"Oh, no!" answered Fix. "I expect to stop at Hong Kong — at least for a few days."

"But how is it that I haven't seen you on board between

Calcutta and here?"

"Oh, I haven't been feeling very well and so stayed in my cabin. And how is your master, Mr Phileas Fogg?"

"He is quite well, thank you, and not a day late in his journey. Ah, Mr Fix; here is something you don't know. We have a young lady with us."

"A young lady?" said Fix, who looked as if he had no idea as to what Passepartout meant.

Passepartout then told him the story. He told him about the adventure in Bombay, the buying of the elephant at the price of two thousand pounds, how they had saved Aouda in the forest, and how they had been stopped at Calcutta.

Fix, who knew all the last part of the story, acted as if he knew nothing at all.

"But," asked Fix, "does your master mean to take this lady to Europe with him?"

"No, Mr Fix, no. We are simply going to put her under the care of her uncle, a rich merchant in Hong Kong."

Fix was disappointed. He had thought that this business of the carrying off of Aouda would give him the chance to make fresh trouble at Hong Kong.

"May I offer you something to drink, Mr Passepartout?"

"Thank you; you may," answered the Frenchman.

After this talk, the detective and Passepartout often met on deck. Fix did not try to get any more information out of his companion and only caught sight of Mr Fogg once or twice as he sat in the cabin talking to Aouda or playing cards.

Passepartout began thinking very seriously about the strange chance that kept Fix with them. And it really was surprising. Here was this very kind gentleman whom he met first at Suez, sailing on the *Mongolia*, getting off at Bombay where he was to stay, then appearing on the *Rangoon* on his way to Hong Kong. In fact, here he was following Mr Fogg step by step. It was worth thinking about. It was most strange. Passepartout felt certain that Fix would leave Hong Kong at the same time as Mr Fogg, and probably by the same steamer.

If Passepartout had thought about the matter for a hundred years he would never have guessed the real reason for which his master was being followed. He would never have imagined that Mr Fogg was being followed round the world as a robber. But as all people like to find an explanation of everything, Passepartout found an explanation that seemed very reasonable. Fix, he felt sure, had been sent by the members of the Reform Club to see that the journey was carried out fairly and according to the agreement.

"It must be that!" said the good fellow, proud at his cleverness. "He has been sent secretly to make sure that my master is not playing any tricks. That is not right. Ah! gentlemen of the Reform Club, you will be sorry for your behaviour!"

Pleased with his discovery, Passepartout made up his mind, all the same, to say nothing to his master about it, fearing that his feelings would be hurt at the distrust shown by his friends. But he promised himself to have little jokes on the subject with Mr Fix. He would pretend that he thought Mr Fix to be a servant of the shipping company.

On Wednesday afternoon, October 30th, the *Rangoon* passed through the Straits of Malacca, which separate the island of Sumatra from the country of the Malays. Beautiful little islands, with their steep mountain sides, hid the view of Sumatra from the passengers.

At four o'clock the next morning the *Rangoon*, having arrived half a day earlier than usual, stopped at Singapore to take in more coal.

Phileas Fogg marked this gain in his notebook and this time went on shore with Aouda, who wished to go for a short walk.

Fix, who distrusted every action of Fogg's, followed him secretly. Passepartout, who was amused to see him doing this, went on shore to buy some fruit.

The island of Singapore is neither large nor striking in appearance. Although it has no mountains it is a very pretty place.

After a pleasant drive of two hours among the woods and hills, Aouda and her companion came back to the town, and at ten o'clock went on board the boat — with the detective, who, of course, had never lost sight of them.

Passepartout was waiting for them on the deck of the *Rangoon*. He had been buying quantities of the fruits of the country, and offered some to Aouda, who was very grateful for them.

At eleven o'clock the *Rangoon*, having taken in its coal, steamed out of the harbour, and a few hours later the passengers could see no more of the high mountains and forests of Malacca.

Thirteen hundred miles separate Singapore from Hong Kong, a small British island lying off the coast of China. Phileas Fogg trusted to spend not more than six days in getting there, so that he could take the boat that left there on November 6th for Yokohama, one of the chief towns of Japan.

The weather, which had been fairly good up to then, changed when the moon went into its last quarter. The sea became rough. At times there was a strong wind, which fortunately blew from the south-east — the right direction for the ship. The captain often raised the sails, and with these and the steam the ship went forward at great speed past the coasts of Annam and Cochin China.

But the ship did not go fast enough to please Passepartout. He felt angry with the captain, the engineer and the shipping company. As for Mr Fogg, he showed no impatience or anxiety at all.

"You seem to be in a great hurry to get to Hong Kong," said Mr Fix to Passepartout one day.

"Yes, in a great hurry," answered Passepartout.

"You think that Mr Fogg is anxious to catch the boat at Yokohama?"

"Terribly anxious."

"Then you believe in this journey round the world?"

"I do. Don't you, Mr Fix?"

"No, I don't!"

"You cunning fellow!" answered Passepartout.

This answer made the detective wonder what he meant. He felt rather uneasy without quite knowing why. Had the Frenchman guessed who he was? He hardly knew what to think. Passepartout could not have guessed his secret, yet what he said certainly meant something.

Another day Passepartout went even further. He could not help saying:

"When we get to Hong Kong, Mr Fix, I wonder whether we shall have the bad fortune to leave you there?"

"Well," answered Fix, not quite knowing what to say. "I hardly know; perhaps ——"

"Ah!" said Passepartout, "if you come with us I shall be very pleased. Come now! As you are a servant of the shipping company you can hardly leave us during the journey, can you? First you were only going as far as Bombay, and now you will soon be in China! America isn't far, and from America to Europe is only a step!"

Fix looked carefully at Passepartout, on whose face there was a most pleasant smile, and decided to treat what he said as a joke. But Passepartout could not stop, and went on:

"Do you get much money for your sort of work?"

"Yes and no," answered Fix. "There are good times and bad. But of course I travel free."

"Oh, I'm sure you do," cried Passepartout with a laugh.

After this talk Fix went back to his cabin and began to think. Passepartout had certainly guessed who he was. In some way or other Passepartout had come to know that he was a detective. But had he told his master? What was Passepartout doing in this business? Was he himself one of the bank robbers? Did Passepartout and his master know everything? In that case he, Fix, had lost the game.

Fix spent several hours worrying about it, sometimes believing that all was lost and sometimes hoping that Fogg knew nothing of the real state of things. He could not make up his mind how to act for the best.

In the end he decided to speak openly to Passepartout. If he could not manage to arrest Fogg at Hong Kong, and if Fogg was not going to stay on that island, he, Fix, would tell Passepartout everything. Either the servant was one of the robbers or he was not. If he was, then Fix could not succeed; if he was not, then it would be to the interest of Passepartout to help Fix to arrest Fogg.

That is how matters stood between those two men, but what about Fogg and Aouda? Passepartout could not make it out. She was clearly very grateful towards the Englishman, but what were Fogg's feelings towards her? He was certainly ready at all times to protect her, but he was certainly not in love with her. And Fogg did not seem to worry at all about his chances of winning or losing the bet; the one who worried was Passepartout. One day he was watching the great engines.

"There isn't enough steam," he cried. "We are not moving! These Englishmen are afraid of using steam. Ah, if this were an American ship, the engines would perhaps burst, but we should move faster!"

During the last days of this journey the weather was rather bad. The wind blew harder and harder from the north-west — which was the wrong direction. The ship rolled in the rough sea, and the passengers were very uncomfortable.

On November 3rd and 4th the sea was rougher still, and the speed grew less. If the wind did not drop, the ship would be at least twenty hours late. In this case, it would be too late to catch the steamer to Yokohama. But Phileas Fogg did not seem to worry at all.

Fix was very pleased. If the *Rangoon* reached Hong Kong after the Yokohama steamer had left, Fogg would have to stay some days on the island. So he welcomed the grey sky and the winds. He was rather seasick, it is true, but that did not matter.

But the impatience of Passepartout can easily be imagined. He stayed on the deck all the time. It was impossible for him to stay below. He climbed up the masts and helped with the sails. He jumped from rope to rope and amused the sailors by his acrobatic tricks. He questioned the captain, the officers and the sailors, who could not help laughing to see his anxiety. He wanted to know exactly how long the bad weather would last.

At last the wind grew less and blew from the right direction. During the day of November 5th the sea grew calmer. Passepartout grew calmer too, as the ship moved faster and faster.

But it was impossible to make up for the lost time. There was no help for it, and land was seen only on the 6th at five o'clock in the morning. Phileas Fogg had expected to reach Hong Kong on the 5th. He was twenty-four hours late. He would certainly not be able to catch the steamer for Yokohama.

At six o'clock the pilot came on board the *Rangoon* and took his place on the bridge so as to guide the ship into the harbour.

Passepartout was most anxious to go and ask him whether the Yokohama steamer had left. But he dared not do so, preferring to keep his hope until the last moment. He had spoken about his fears to Fix, who tried to comfort him.

"There is nothing to worry about," he said. "If your master does not catch the boat for Yokohama, he has only to take the next one."

This answer made Passepartout violently angry.

But if Passepartout dared not question the pilot, Mr Fogg went and asked him when a boat would leave Hong Kong for Yokohama.

"Tomorrow morning," answered the pilot.

"Ah," said Mr Fogg, without showing any surprise.

Passepartout heard these words, and wanted to throw his arms lovingly round the pilot's neck. Fix heard the answer too, but he would have preferred to break the pilot's neck.

"What is the name of the steamer?" asked Mr Fogg.

"The *Carnatic*," answered the pilot.

"But wasn't the *Carnatic* to leave yesterday?"

"Yes, sir, but one of its boilers had to be repaired, and so the boat will not start until tomorrow."

"Thank you," answered Mr Fogg, and went down below.

Passepartout took the pilot's hand and shook it with violence, saying, "You are a splendid fellow!"

The pilot probably never knew why Passepartout was so pleased with him, and went on with his duties.

At one o'clock the *Rangoon* reached the quay, and the passengers landed.

It must be said that Phileas Fogg had been exceptionally fortunate. Without the accident to its boiler the *Carnatic* would have left Hong Kong the day before, and passengers for Japan would have had to wait a week for the next ship. Mr Fogg was twenty-four hours late but this would not be a very serious matter. The steamer from Yokohama to San Francisco would have to wait for the *Carnatic*, it is true, but no doubt it would be easy to make up for the twenty-four hours during the crossing of the Pacific.

So except for these twenty-four hours, Mr Fogg found himself in agreement with the plan that he had made in London thirty-five days earlier.

8

Passepartout Drinks Too Much

The *Carnatic* was to leave the next morning at five o'clock. So Mr Fogg had sixteen hours before him during which time he could do his business — that is to say, take Aouda to her uncle and leave her with him.

Mr Fogg, the lady, and Passepartout landed, and a little later found themselves at the Club Hotel. Leaving Aouda in her room, Fogg went off to find the Indian uncle in whose care he would leave her. At the same time he ordered Passepartout to stay at the hotel so that the lady would not be left alone.

Mr Fogg paid a visit to one of the chief business houses of the town, where he was certain that the Honourable Mr Jejeeh, Aouda's uncle, would be known. But here he received the information that this rich Indian merchant had given up his business two years before. He had made his fortune and had gone to live in Europe — in Holland, it was thought.

Phileas Fogg went back to the Club Hotel. He asked to see Aouda and told her that her uncle was no longer in Hong Kong and that he had probably gone to live in Holland.

Aouda did not answer at once. She passed a few moments in thought and then asked:

"What shall I do, Mr Fogg?"

"It is quite simple. Come to Europe."

"But I can't give you so much trouble."

"It is no trouble at all. Passepartout!"

"Yes, sir," answered his servant.

"Go to the *Carnatic* and ask for three cabins."

Passepartout went off to do so, very pleased to think that they would not lose the company of the young Indian lady.

At the harbour he saw Fix walking up and down the quay with a look of disappointment on his face.

There was a good reason for him to be disappointed; the warrant for the arrest of Mr Fogg had not reached Hong Kong. It was certainly on the way, but it would come too late. From Hong Kong onwards Fogg would be outside the reach of English law, and so could not be arrested. If Fix could not keep him for a few days in Hong Kong, he would escape.

"Good!" thought Passepartout to himself. "Things are not going well for the gentlemen of the Reform Club."

He went up to Fix with a pleasant smile.

"Well, Mr Fix, have you decided to come with us as far as America?" asked Passepartout.

"Yes," answered Fix between his teeth.

Passepartout burst out laughing.

"I knew it!" he cried. "I was certain that you could not separate yourself from us. Come and order a cabin."

They went into the office of the shipping company and ordered cabins for four people. The man at the office pointed out that as the repairs to the *Carnatic* had already been finished, the ship would leave that evening at eight o'clock, and not the next morning, as had been arranged.

"Very good," answered Passepartout. "That will suit my master. I will go and warn him."

At that moment Fix came to a decision. He would tell Passepartout everything. It was the only way to keep Phileas Fogg some days at Hong Kong.

On leaving the office, Fix said:

"You have plenty of time. Let's go and have something to drink."

"Very well," answered Passepartout, "but we mustn't stay long."

They went into a sort of drinking hall. At the end of the room there was a big bed on which several people were lying asleep. There were about thirty people here sitting at tables and drinking.

Fix and Passepartout sat down, and Fix ordered two bottles of wine. The Frenchman, finding it to his taste, drank a glass — two glasses, three, and more. Fix drank little, and watched his companion closely. They talked of different things, and particularly of this good idea of Fix joining them on the *Carnatic*. Talking of this steamer made Passepartout remember that he must go and tell his master about the change in the hour of sailing. He got up.

"Stop a moment," said Fix.

"Well, what is it, Mr Fix?"

"I have something serious to tell you."

"Something serious!" cried Passepartout, drinking the last of the wine. "Well, we will talk about it tomorrow. I haven't time today."

"Wait," said Fix. "It's about your master."

Passepartout looked at Fix, and seeing the strange look on his face, sat down again.

"What have you got to tell me?" asked Passepartout.

Fix laid his hand on his companion's arm and, lowering his voice, said:

"You have guessed who I am?"

"Of course I have!" answered Passepartout, smiling.

"Then I will tell you everything ——"

"Now that I know everything! Very good! However, go on. But let me first tell you that these gentlemen are spending their money needlessly."

"Needlessly!" said Fix. "It is easy to see that you do not know how much money —— "

"Yes, I do. Twenty thousand pounds."

"No, fifty-five thousand pounds," answered Fix.

"What!" cried Passepartout! "Fifty-five thousand pounds! Well, that is a greater reason why I should not lose a moment," he added, as he got up again.

"Yes, fifty-five thousand pounds!" answered Fix, who forced Passepartout to sit down again. He ordered another bottle, but this time, of a drink much stronger than wine.

"And if I succeed, I shall get two thousand pounds for myself. And listen to me: if you help me, I will give you half of that. Will you accept a thousand pounds for helping me?"

"Helping you?" cried Passepartout with his eyes very wide open.

"Yes, for helping me to keep Mr Fogg for some days in Hong Kong."

"What's that!" cried Passepartout. "What are you saying? What! Is it not enough to have my master followed, to have doubts about him? And now these gentlemen want to put difficulties in his way! I am ashamed of them!"

"What do you mean? What are you talking about?" asked Fix, who understood nothing of what Passepartout was saying.

"I mean this, that it is dishonesty, pure dishonesty! You might as well take money out of Mr Fogg's pocket!"

"That's just what we are hoping to do!" answered Fix.

"But it's a trick!" cried Passepartout, who had been drinking glass after glass from the new bottle, not noticing in his excitement what he was doing. "It's a trick, I tell you, a wicked trick! 'Gentlemen' they call themselves!"

Fix understood less and less.

"Friends!" cried Passepartout. "Fellow members of the Reform Club. Let me tell you, Mr Fix, that my master is an honest man, and that when he bets he expects to win his bet honestly."

"But who do you think I am?" asked Fix.

"Who you are?" answered Passepartout. "Why you are a man sent by the members of the Reform Club, to keep watch over my master — a piece of work of which they ought to be ashamed! Oh, for some time past I have known who you are, and I have taken good care not to say anything to my master about it!"

"He knows nothing?" asked Fix.

"Nothing," answered Passepartout, emptying his glass again.

The detective began to think hard. He said nothing for a few moments. What should he do? Passepartout's mistake made the detective's plan more difficult. It was clear that Passepartout was perfectly honest and open, that he had nothing to do with the robbery — which Fix had feared.

"Well," he thought, "as he has had nothing to do with the robbery, he will help me."

The detective made up his mind for the second time. Besides, there was no time to be lost. He *must* arrest Fogg at Hong Kong.

"Listen," said Fix. "Listen to me carefully. I am not what you think; I have not been sent by the members of the Reform Club."

"I don't believe you!" said Passepartout.

"I am a detective sent by the London police."

"You! A London detective!"

"Yes, and I can prove it. Look at my papers."

Saying this, he took his papers from his pocketbook and showed them to his companion. The papers were signed by the chief of police. Passepartout looked at them and then at Fix, too surprised to say a word.

"This bet," said Fix, "is only a trick. By betting that he would go round the world in eighty days he made you and the members of the Reform Club help him to escape from the police."

"Escape? Why should he want to escape from the police? What has he done?"

"Listen," said Fix. "On September the 28th, last, fifty-five thousand pounds were stolen from the Bank of England. We have the description of the man who stole it. Here is the description. It is exactly that of your master, point by point."

"Impossible," cried Passepartout, striking the table. "My master is the most honest man in the world!"

"How do you know that?" said Fix. "You don't even know him. You became his servant on the day he left England, and he left in a great hurry, and without any luggage. The only reason he gave for leaving was this foolish bet. And he took with him an immense sum of money. Do you mean to tell me that he is an honest man?"

"Yes, yes, I do," answered the poor fellow.

"As you helped him to escape, you will be arrested too. You know that?"

Passepartout was holding his head between his hands. His face was quite changed. He dared not look at the detective. What? Phileas Fogg a thief? He, the good man who had so bravely saved Aouda? But he had acted exactly as a thief would act, and appearances were against him. Passepartout tried not to believe what Fix had said. He refused to think that his master was guilty. However, he had drunk so much that it was difficult for him to think clearly.

"Well, what do you want me to do?" he asked the detective at last.

"Listen," answered Fix. "I have followed Mr Fogg as far as here, but I have not yet received the warrant for his arrest. So you must help me to prevent him from leaving Hong Kong."

"Help you to keep him here?"

"Yes, and I will divide with you the two thousand pounds promised by the Bank of England."

"Never!" cried Passepartout, who tried to stand up. But he fell back in his chair, feeling both his strength and his reason leaving him.

"Mr Fix," he said, making every effort to speak. "Even . . . even if what you tell me is true . . . even if he is the thief . . . the thief you are looking for . . . and that's not true . . . I am in his service . . . I have seen him as a good and brave man . . . What? Help you to catch him? . . . Never! . . . Not for all the gold in the world . . . I'm not the sort of man to do that sort of thing!"

"You refuse?"

"I refuse."

"All right. Forget that I have said anything to you," said Fix. "Drink this; it will do you good."

Saying this the detective poured a full glass out of the bottle and made the Frenchman drink it.

This was all that was needed to finish Passepartout. He was no longer able to speak. He fell heavily from his chair and lay on the ground without any movement.

"Good," thought Fix. "Mr Fogg will not be warned of the changed hour of the sailing of the *Carnatic*, and if he does leave, he will at least leave without the company of this troublesome Frenchman!"

Then he paid for the drink and went out.

9

Mr Fogg Misses the Boat

While all this was happening, Mr Fogg and Aouda were having a walk in the town. Since Aouda had accepted his offer to take her to Europe, he had been thinking of what would be needed for her journey. An Englishman such as he might go round the world with no other luggage but a handbag, but it was not the same case with a lady. So it was necessary to buy clothes for her, and all sorts of other things needed for travelling. Mr Fogg saw to everything with his usual calmness, and when the young woman said he was being too kind to her, he said:

"All this is a part of my plan. Please say no more."

Having bought all the things needed, Mr Fogg and the young woman went back to the hotel, where they were served with a splendid dinner. Then Aouda, who was rather tired, went to her room.

Mr Fogg spent the whole evening reading the newspapers.

If he were a man who was ever surprised at anything, he would have been surprised at not seeing Passepartout come back. But knowing that the *Carnatic* would not leave Hong Kong until the next morning, he did not think of the matter any more. But the next morning Passepartout did not answer the bell when he rang for him.

Nobody knows what Mr Fogg thought when he was told that his servant had not come back. However, he took up his bag, called Aouda and ordered a carriage to take them to the quay.

It was then eight o'clock, and the *Carnatic* was to leave at half past nine.

When the carriage came to the door of the hotel, Mr Fogg and Aouda took their seats in it. Half an hour later they reached the quay, and then Mr Fogg was informed that the *Carnatic* had left the night before.

Mr Fogg had expected to find both the boat and his servant, and now he had to do without either of them. But no look of disappointment was to be seen on his face, and as Aouda looked anxiously at him he simply answered:

"It's nothing. It doesn't matter."

At that moment somebody who had been watching them came up to him. It was the detective Fix, who said good morning, and then asked:

"Were you not one of my fellow-passengers on the *Rangoon* that came in yesterday?"

"Yes, sir," answered Mr Fogg coldly, "but I have not the honour of knowing you."

"Excuse me, but I expected to find your servant here."

"Do you know where he is?" asked the lady.

"What!" answered Fix. "Isn't he with you?"

"No," answered Aouda. We have not seen him since yesterday. Has he perhaps sailed on the *Carnatic*?"

"Without you? That is hardly possible," answered the detective. "But excuse my question, were you expecting to leave by the *Carnatic*?"

"Yes."

"I, too, was expecting to leave by it, and I am very disappointed. The *Carnatic*, having completed its repairs, left Hong Kong twelve hours earlier without warning anybody, and now we must wait a week for the next steamer."

In saying the words "a week" Fix felt himself filled with joy. A week! Fogg staying a week in Hong Kong. There would be time to receive the warrant. In other words, fortune smiled on the officer of the law.

He did not feel so happy when he heard the next words of Phileas Fogg.

"But there seem to be other ships than the *Carnatic* in Hong Kong harbour."

Mr Fogg, offering his arm to Aouda, went off to find a ship that might be leaving. Fix followed them.

But fortune was against Mr Fogg. For three hours he walked up and down the quays by the harbour. He was ready to hire a ship to take them to Yokohama, but found none. Fix began to hope again.

Mr Fogg, however, did not give up his plan. He would even go as far as Macao to find a ship if necessary. A sailor came up to him.

"Are you looking for a boat, sir?" he asked.

"You have a boat ready to sail?" asked Mr Fogg.

"Yes, sir, a pilot-boat, number 43, the best of them all."

"Is it a fast boat?"

"Between eight and nine miles an hour. Would you like to see it?"

"Yes."

"You shall. Do you want to go for a sail?"

"I want to go to Yokohama."

The sailor opened his eyes and mouth wide.

"You are joking, sir."

"No. I couldn't catch the *Carnatic*, and I must be in Yokohama by the 14th at the latest so as to catch the steamer for San Francisco."

"I'm sorry," said the pilot, "but it's impossible."

"I offer you a hundred pounds a day, and two hundred pounds more if I get there in time."

"Do you mean it?"

"I mean it."

The pilot walked off for a few moments to think. He looked at the sea, his feelings torn between the wish to earn such a large sum of money and the fear of going so far in a small boat. Fix waited in a state of the greatest anxiety.

During this time Mr Fogg had turned towards Aouda.

"You will not be afraid?" he asked.

"With you, no, Mr Fogg," she answered.

The pilot came up again.

"Well, pilot?" said Mr Fogg.

"Well, sir, I cannot put my life into danger, nor those of my men, nor yours, on such a long journey in a small boat and at this time of the year. Besides, we shall not get there in time, for it is 1,650 miles from Hong Kong to Yokohama."

"Only 1,600," said Mr Fogg.

"It's the same thing."

Fix breathed again.

"But," added the pilot, "there may be another way out of the difficulty."

"And what is that?" asked Phileas Fogg.

"By going to Nagasaki, in the south of Japan, eleven hundred miles, or to Shanghai, eight hundred miles from Hong Kong. By going to Shanghai we should keep along the coast of China, which would be safer; and besides that, the winds blow in that direction at this time of the year."

"Pilot," answered Phileas Fogg, "I am to take the American steamer at Yokohama, and not at Shanghai or at Nagasaki."

"Why not?" answered the pilot. "The San Francisco steamer does not start from Yokohama. It stops there and at Nagasaki, but it really starts its journey at Shanghai."

"Are you sure?"

"Quite."

"And when does the steamer leave Shanghai?"

"On the 11th at seven o'clock in the evening. So we have four days before us. Four days, that's ninety-six hours, and at the speed of eight miles an hour, which is possible with a good wind; and if the sea is calm we can do the eight hundred miles that separate us from Shanghai."

"And you can leave —— ?"

"In an hour. I need only enough time to get the food on board and the sails raised."

"Very well. I agree. Are you the master of the boat?"

"Yes. John Bunsby, master of the *Tankadere*."

"Shall I give part of the money now?"

"If you don't mind."

"Here are two hundred pounds. Sir," added Phileas Fogg, turning towards Fix, "if you would like to join us —— "

"Sir," answered Fix, "I was going to ask you to take me."

"Very well. In half an hour we shall be on board."

"But poor Passepartout," said Aouda, who was very anxious at the disappearance of the servant.

"I will do all I can for him," answered Phileas Fogg.

And while Fix, in a very bad temper, was going to the boat, the two others went to the police station of Hong Kong. There Phileas Fogg gave a description of Passepartout and left enough money to send him back to Europe. Then calling at the hotel to get the luggage again, they went off to the boat.

Three o'clock struck. Pilot-boat number 43 was ready to raise its sails.

Besides John Bunsby there were four men on the boat, four

strong and clever sailors who knew the China Sea perfectly. John Bunsby, a man about forty-five years old, with sharp eyes and an active body, was a man whom anyone could trust.

Phileas and Aouda went on board. Fix was already there. They went down into a small, but clean, cabin.

"I am sorry not to be able to offer you anything better than this," said Mr Fogg to Fix, who bowed without answering.

The detective did not feel happy at having to accept the kind offer of Mr Fogg.

"He's a very polite thief," thought Fix, "but he is a thief, all the same."

At ten minutes past three the sails were raised. The travellers were sitting on the deck, and Mr Fogg and Aouda looked at the quay for the last time in case Passepartout should appear.

Fix was not without some fear. The unfortunate fellow whom he had treated so badly might yet come, and then there would be an explanation not at all to the liking of the detective. But the Frenchman did not appear. No doubt he was still suffering from what he had been given to drink.

Then John Bunsby threw off the ropes, and the *Tankadere* made its way at great speed towards the north.

10

The Storm

This journey of eight hundred miles on a ship of this sort was not without danger. The China Seas are generally rough, particularly at this time of the year. As the pilot was being paid by the day, he would certainly have earned more money by going to Yokohama. The journey to Shanghai was already dangerous enough.

During the long hours of this day, the *Tankadere* made its way through the narrow necks of water to the north of Hong Kong.

"I hardly need tell you, pilot," said Phileas Fogg, as the boat reached the open sea, "how important it is to go as fast as possible."

"Trust to me," answered John Bunsby. "We are carrying as much sail as the wind will allow us to do."

"Well, it's your business, pilot, and not mine. I trust to you."

Phileas Fogg, standing up straight like a sailor, fearlessly watched the rough waves. The young woman, seated near him, was looking, too, at the dark green water as it rushed by, thinking, no doubt, of her future. Above her floated the white sails, and the ship flew forward as a bird flies through the air.

Night came. The moon was in its first quarter, and its light would soon no longer be seen. Clouds were coming up from the east and already covered a good part of the sky.

Fix was in the front part of the ship. He kept away from the others, knowing that Fogg disliked talking. Besides, he did not care to talk to the man from whom he had accepted so much kindness. He, too, was thinking of the future. He felt certain that Fogg would not stop at Yokohama, but would at once take the San Francisco boat for America, where he would be safe. It seemed to him a good plan.

Instead of leaving England straight for America, as most people in his place would have done, he preferred to sail round three-quarters of the earth so as to reach America still more safely. There, having successfully escaped from the police, he would spend the money that he had stolen. But what would Fix do when they reached America? Would he give up following his man? No, a hundred times no! He would follow him until he caught him. It was his duty, and he would do his duty to the end. In any case one fortunate thing had happened. Passepartout was no longer with his master and after what Fix had said to him, it was important that master and servant should meet no more.

Phileas Fogg, too, was thinking about his servant who had

disappeared in such a strange way. Perhaps he had, after all, managed to sail on the *Carnatic*. Aouda, too, thought it possible. She was very sorry to lose this faithful servant, to whom she owed her life. They might, then, find him at Yokohama, and it should not be difficult to discover whether the *Carnatic* had taken him there or not.

At about ten o'clock the wind grew stronger.

At midnight Phileas Fogg and Aouda went down to the cabin. Fix was already there and asleep. The pilot and his men stayed on the deck all night.

By the next day, November 8th, the boat had gone more than a hundred miles. Its speed was between eight and nine miles an hour. There was plenty of wind in the sails, and at this rate, the boat had every chance of doing the distance in good time.

During this day the *Tankadere* kept close to the coast, and the sea was running in the right direction.

Mr Fogg and the young woman, neither of whom suffered from seasickness, enjoyed a good meal. Fix was asked to join them, and had to accept, but he did not like accepting. To have Fogg pay for his journey and his meals seemed too much — it did not seem to him quite fair — but all the same he had his meal.

But at the end of the meal he took Mr Fogg on one side and said:

"Sir."

He did not like saying "sir" to this thief that he was going to arrest.

"Sir, you have been kind enough to offer me a passage on this boat. But although I am not rich enough to pay as much as what I should like, let me ——"

"We will not speak of that, sir," answered Mr Fogg.

"But, please ——"

"No, sir," said Fogg. "I count that as part of the cost of my journey."

Fix bowed, and said no more during the whole day.

The ship sailed well. John Bunsby had good hopes. More than once he said to Mr Fogg that they would get to Shanghai in time.

Mr Fogg simply answered that that was what he expected. Thinking of the rich reward they would receive, the sailors worked hard.

That evening they were two hundred miles from Hong Kong and Phileas Fogg had every reason to hope that they would reach Yokohama in plenty of time.

Early in the morning the *Tankadere* was sailing between the island of Formosa and the coast of China. The sea was very rough at this point, and the movements of the ship were so violent that the travellers had some difficulty in standing up. When the sun rose the wind blew more strongly and the sky was covered with black clouds.

The pilot looked at the sky. He was feeling anxious.

"Do you mind if I tell you the truth?" he asked Fogg.

"Tell me everything," answered Fogg.

"Well, we are going to have a storm."

"Is it coming from the south or north?"

"From the south."

"That is splendid, then, for it will blow us in the right direction," said Mr Fogg.

"If that is how you think about the matter, I have nothing more to say," answered the pilot.

John Bunsby was right. Those storms of the China Sea at this time of the year were severe. All the sails except one were taken down. All the doors and other openings were fastened so that no water could come in. They waited.

John Bunsby had begged his passengers to go down below, but it would not have been pleasant to be shut up in the cabin, where there was little air, so they preferred to stay on deck.

About eight o'clock the storm broke. Rain poured down. Even with one sail the ship flew over the water. All that day the waves poured over the deck. When evening came the wind changed its direction and began to blow from the north-west. The waves struck the side of the ship and made it roll terribly. It was fortunate that the *Tankadere* was so solidly built.

As night came the storm grew more violent. John Bunsby and

his men felt very anxious. The pilot went up to Mr Fogg and said:

"I think, sir, that we had better try to find a harbour."

"I think so, too," answered Phileas Fogg.

"But which one?"

"I know only of one."

"And which is that?"

"Shanghai."

It took the pilot a few moments to understand what this answer meant. Then he said:

"Very well, sir, you are right. Let us go to Shanghai."

And so the *Tankadere* kept on its way to the north, but more slowly.

It was a terrible night. It was a wonder that the ship did not sink. More than once Mr Fogg rushed to Aouda to protect her from the waves.

At last daylight came. The storm was still violent, but the wind changed to the south-east. This was better, and the ship flew forward again. Sometimes the coast of China was to be seen, but no ships. The *Tankadere* was alone on the sea.

At midday the sea was a little calmer, and when the sun went down the wind blew less violently. The travellers were now able to take a little food and to rest.

The night was fairly calm. The pilot put up more sails. The ship moved at a good speed. The next morning, the 11th, John Bunsby was able to say that they were not more than a hundred miles from Shanghai.

A hundred miles, and there was only this one day in which to sail the distance. If they were to catch the steamer for Yokohama, they must reach Shanghai that same evening. Without the storm, during which they had lost several hours, they would now have been only thirty miles away.

The wind blew much less strongly, but fortunately the sea grew calmer at the same time. All the sails were put up. At midday the *Tankadere* was not more than forty-five miles from Shanghai. Only six hours were left in which to catch the boat. All those on the ship feared that the time was too short. It was necessary to sail at the speed of nine miles an hour, but the wind was weakening all the time. The ship, however, was light and fast; the sails picked up the little wind there was, and so at six o'clock John Bunsby found himself not more than ten miles from Shanghai River, for the town itself is twelve miles from the mouth of the river.

At seven o'clock they were three miles away. A violent word escaped from the mouth of the pilot. He was certainly going to lose his reward of two hundred pounds. He looked at Mr Fogg. Mr Fogg was perfectly calm, and yet his whole fortune was in danger.

At that moment a long black chimney came into sight. Black smoke was pouring out of it. It was the American steamer sailing from Shanghai at its usual time.

"Make signals," said Phileas Fogg.

A small brass cannon was on deck. It was used to make signals during foggy weather.

John Bunsby filled the cannon with gunpowder.

"Fire!" said Mr Fogg.

And the roar of the cannon was heard.

11

Passepartout Has No Money

The *Carnatic* left Hong Kong on November 7th, at half past six in the evening, and went at full steam towards Japan. It carried many passengers. There were two empty cabins — those that should have been used by Mr Fogg.

The next morning the men on deck saw with some surprise a passenger with an unwashed face and hair in disorder come out from his cabin, climb on deck, and fall into a chair. It was

Passepartout. This is what had happened.

A few moments after Fix had left the drinking hall, two Chinese saw Passepartout sleeping on the floor. They lifted him up and laid him on the bed among the other sleeping men. But three hours later, remembering even in his dreams that there was a duty that he had left undone, the poor fellow woke up and fought against his sleepiness and the poison of the drink in his blood. He got up. Half-walking and half-crawling, holding himself up by keeping close to the walls, he managed to find his way into the street.

"The *Carnatic*, the *Carnatic*," he cried, as if in a dream.

With difficulty he made his way to the quay. The steamer was there with smoke pouring out of its chimneys. Passepartout climbed on board, and fell to the deck senseless, when the ship started.

Some men of the crew, used to seeing this sort of thing, carried him down to a cabin, and Passepartout slept until the following morning at a hundred and fifty miles from Hong Kong.

That is how it was, then, that he found himself on the deck of the *Carnatic*. The fresh air brought him to his senses. He began to remember, but with some difficulty, what had happened to him the night before: the drinking-hall, what Fix had told him, and all the rest.

"I must have been terribly drunk," he thought. "What will Mr Fogg say to me? Anyhow, I have caught the boat, and that is the chief thing."

Then he thought about Fix.

"We shall see no more of him, I hope. After what he said to me he will not dare follow us on the *Carnatic*. A police-detective, he calls himself, a detective wanting to arrest my master for stealing money from the Bank of England!"

Passepartout began wondering whether he should tell the story to his master. Ought he to let him know about Fix? Would it not be better to wait until they got to London, and then to tell him how a detective had followed him round the world? What a joke that would be! Yes, that would be the best thing to do. Anyhow, he would decide that later. The most important thing now was to go and join his master and beg pardon for his behaviour of the night before.

So Passepartout got up from his chair. The sea was rather rough and the boat was rolling heavily. The good fellow walked as well as he could, went up and down the deck, but saw nobody at all like Mr Fogg or Aouda.

"Very well," he thought. "The lady has probably not got up yet, and Mr Fogg has probably found somebody to play cards with."

So he went down to the hall. Mr Fogg was not there. He then went to the office to ask which was Mr Fogg's cabin. The man at the office said that there was nobody of that name on the boat.

"But excuse me," said Passepartout. "He must be on the boat." He then gave the officer a description of Mr Fogg, saying that with him there was a young lady.

"We have no young ladies on board," answered the officer. "Here is a list of passengers; you can see for yourself."

Passepartout looked at the list. The name of his master was not there. A sudden idea struck him.

"Am I on the *Carnatic*?"

"Yes," answered the officer.

"On the way to Yokohama?"

"Certainly."

Passepartout had been afraid for a moment that he was on the wrong boat. But if he was on the *Carnatic*, it was certain that his master was not.

Then he remembered everything. He remembered how the hour of sailing had been changed, that he was going to warn his master and that he had not done so. It was his fault, then, that Mr Fogg and his companion had not caught the boat!

His fault, yes. But it was still more the fault of the man who, to keep his master in Hong Kong, had taken him to the drinking hall and had made him drunk. And now Mr Fogg had certainly lost his bet; he was perhaps arrested; he might even be in prison! At this thought he tore his hair. Ah! if ever he got hold of Fix, how he would pay him out for his cunning and trickery!

When the first terrible moments of his discovery had passed, Passepartout grew calmer and began to examine his position. It was not a happy one. He was on his way to Japan. He was certain to get there, but how would he get away from it? His pockets were empty. He had no money at all. It is true that his cabin and food had been paid for, so that he had five or six days in front of him and during this time he could make some plan for the future.

It is impossible to describe how much he ate and drank during this part of the journey. He ate and drank for his master, for Aouda and for himself. He ate as if Japan were a country in which there was no food at all.

On the morning of the 13th, the *Carnatic* reached Yokohama, and tied up to the quay among a large number of ships that had come from nearly all the countries in the world.

Passepartout, feeling rather frightened, landed in this strange Land of the Rising Sun. All that he could do was to be guided by chance and go walking about the streets. He first found himself in the European part of the town where, as at Hong Kong, the streets were crowded with people of all countries, Americans, English, Chinese; merchants willing to buy or to sell anything. Among all these people Passepartout felt as lonely as if he had been thrown into the middle of Africa.

There was certainly one thing that he could do. He could go to the French and British consuls, but he very much disliked the idea of telling his story and the story of his master. He would go to the consuls only if everything else failed.

He then went to the Japanese part of the town, where he saw the temples and strangely-built houses. The streets here, too, were crowded with people: priests; officers dressed in silk and carrying two swords; soldiers with their blue and white coats, carrying guns; fishermen, beggars, and large numbers of children.

Passepartout walked about among these people for some

hours, looking at the strange sights, the shops, the eating houses and amusement halls. In the shop, however, he could see neither meat nor bread; and if he had seen any, he had no money. So he decided to go without supper.

The next morning he felt very tired and hungry. He would certainly have to eat something, and the sooner the better. He could, of course, have sold his watch, but he would rather die of hunger than do that.

Now was the time when he could use the strong, if not very musical, voice that nature had given him. He knew a few French and English songs, and he made up his mind to try them.

It was perhaps rather early in the day to start singing, however. It might be better to wait a few hours. The thought then came to his mind that he was too well dressed for a street singer. He would do well to change his clothes for others more suitable for his position. Besides, by so doing he might get a little money with which to buy food.

It was some time before he could find a shop where they bought and sold old clothes. In the end he found one. The owner of the shop liked the look of what Passepartout was wearing, and soon Passepartout came out dressed in Japanese clothes — old ones, it is true, but quite comfortable. What pleased him most were the few pieces of silver money that were the result of the arrangement.

The next thing that Passepartout did was to go to a small eating house, where he was able to satisfy his hunger.

"Now," he thought, "I have no time to lose. I had better make my stay in this Land of the Sun as short as possible."

His idea was to visit any steamers going to America. He could offer his services as cook or servant, asking for nothing except his food and passage. If he could get to San Francisco, he could get on all right. The important thing was to cross the 4,700 miles of sea that lay between Japan and the New World. So he went towards the harbour.

But as he got near the quays, his plan, which had seemed so simple when he made it, now seemed to be more and more impossible to carry out. Why would they need a cook or a servant on an American boat, and what would any captain or officer think of him, dressed as he was? Then again he had no papers to show, no letters from people whom he had served before.

While he was thinking matters over he saw in front of a sort of amusement hall an immense noticeboard:

William Batulcar's
Company of Japanese Acrobats

———

Last Appearances
before leaving for America
of the
Long Noses! Long Noses!
Come and see them!

"America!" cried Passepartout. "Just what I wanted."

He went inside the building and asked for Mr Batulcar. Mr Batulcar appeared.

"What do you want?" he asked, mistaking Passepartout for a Japanese.

"Do you want a servant?" asked Passepartout.

"A servant," cried the man. "I have two strong and faithful servants who have always been with me, who serve me for nothing except food. And here they are!" he added, showing two immensely strong arms.

"So I can be of no help to you?"

"None."

"That's a pity. It would have suited me to go with you to America."

"Oh," answered Mr Batulcar, "you are no more a Japanese than I am. Why are you dressed like that?"

"A man dresses as he can!"

"That's true. You are a Frenchman?"

"Yes."

"Then I suppose you can make funny faces."

"Well," answered Passepartout, who did not at all like this question, "we Frenchmen can certainly make funny faces, but not funnier than American faces!"

"Quite right. Are you strong?"

"Yes."

"Can you sing?"

"Yes."

"Can you sing while you are standing upside-down?"

"Oh, yes," answered Passepartout, thinking of the acrobatic tricks he did when he was young.

"Very well, then, I will take you."

So Passepartout had found a position. He was to serve with this company of Japanese acrobats. It was not a very pleasant way of earning his living, but in a week's time he would be on his way to San Francisco.

At three o'clock that afternoon the hall was filled with the people who had come to see the actors and acrobats do their wonderful tricks. One of the most amusing acts was that of the company of long noses. Each of the players had fastened in front of his face a piece of wood which gave the appearance of an immensely long nose. One of the things they had to do was to form a pyramid with their bodies. But instead of climbing on each other's shoulders, as is usual, the artists were to group themselves on top of the noses. One of the most important positions was that of the middle of the bottom pyramid, for this particular nose supported most of the weight of the people above him. Now the man who had always been in this position had suddenly left the company, so Passepartout had been chosen to take his place.

He felt rather sad when he put on the fine dress that he was to wear — it made him think of when he was young — and when the long nose was fitted to his face. But then, as this nose was going to earn for him something to eat, he felt happier.

Passepartout came in with the others and they all stretched themselves on the ground with their noses sticking up in the air. A second group came and stood on the noses. A third group took their positions on the noses of the others, then came a fourth, until the pyramid reached the top of the hall. The music began to play.

Great was the admiration of all who were watching this, when suddenly the pyramid began to shake. It broke; it fell!

It was the fault of Passepartout. Leaving his important position, he jumped down among the people and fell at the feet of a gentleman standing there. He cried out:

"Ah! my master! my master!"

"You?"

"Yes, I."

"Well, in that case, let us go to the steamer."

Mr Fogg, Aouda, who was with him, and Passepartout quickly went outside, where they found Mr Batulcar violently angry. He wanted to be paid for the breaking of the pyramid. Phileas Fogg calmed him down by giving him a number of bank-notes. And at half past six, at the moment it was going to leave, Mr Fogg and Aouda went on board the American steamer, followed by Passepartout with his six-foot nose still sticking on his face!

It will be understood what had happened at Shanghai. The signals made by the *Tankadere* had been noticed by the Yokohama steamer. The captain, hearing the noise of the cannon and thinking that help was needed, went towards the little ship. A few moments later, Phileas Fogg paid John Bunsby the money that had been promised and gave him in addition five hundred and fifty pounds. Then Mr Fogg and Aouda and Fix climbed on the steamer, which then made its way first to Nagasaki then to Yokohama.

Arrived there that very morning, November 14th, Phileas Fogg at once went on board the *Carnatic*. There he received the information, to the great joy of Aouda and perhaps to his own, that Passepartout had come by that boat and had reached Yokohama the night before.

Phileas Fogg, who was to leave that evening for San Francisco, began at once to look for his servant. He went, but without success, to the French and English consuls. He walked about the streets of Yokohama and, having almost lost hope of finding Passepartout, went almost by chance into Mr Batulcar's hall. Passepartout even in his upside-down position, saw him at once. In his excitement he could not keep his nose from moving. The result of the movement was the fall of the pyramid.

All this Passepartout heard from Aouda, who told him of their journey from Hong Kong to Yokohama in the company of a Mr Fix.

When he heard the name of Fix, Passepartout made no sign. He thought that the moment had not yet come to tell his master what had passed between the police-detective and himself. So in the story of his adventures he said that he had had too much drink in a drinking hall in Hong Kong.

Mr Fogg listened to the story coldly and did not answer. Then he gave enough money to his servant for him to get some new clothes. Passepartout was able to buy clothes on the ship, and an hour later he looked very different from the long-nosed actor of Yokohama.

12

Crossing the Pacific Ocean

The boat carrying them from Yokohama to San Francisco was the *General Grant*, belonging to an American Steamship Company. It was a large steamer, well built and of great speed. At the rate of twelve miles an hour it would take only twenty-one days to cross the Pacific Ocean. Phileas Fogg then had every reason to believe that he would be at San Francisco on December 2nd, at New York on the 11th, and reach London on the 20th, a few hours earlier than the 21st.

There were a good number of people on the boat, English, Americans, and others.

During the crossing nothing particular happened. The sea was calm. Mr Fogg was calm, too, and said little, as usual. Aouda came to respect more and more this man who had done so much for her. In fact, almost without her knowing it, her feelings of respect were changed into feelings of a different sort.

Besides this, she was very interested in this gentleman's plan, and most anxious that nothing might happen to spoil it. She often had talks with Passepartout who soon saw the state of her feelings towards Mr Fogg. He praised his master, his honesty and kindness. Then he comforted her as to the result of the journey, saying that the most difficult part was already over. They had left strange countries like China and Japan, and now by crossing America by train and the Atlantic Ocean by steamer it would be easy to complete the journey round the world in good time.

Nine days after leaving Yokohama Phileas Fogg had gone round exactly one half of the world. It is true that out of the eighty days Mr Fogg had spent fifty-two, and he had only twenty-eight more to spend. But we must note that if that gentleman had done half the journey as measured by the sun, he had really done more than two-thirds in distance as measured by the number of miles travelled. From London to Aden, Aden to Bombay, Calcutta to Singapore, from Singapore to Yokohama — that was a very indirect journey. If we could go round the world as the sun does, the distance from London to London would be 12,000 miles. But by this indirect journey the distance is 26,000 miles, of which Mr Fogg had travelled 17,500. From now onwards, however, the journey would be almost in a straight line. And Fix was no longer there to stop him.

It happened, too, that on this day, November 23rd, Passepartout made a discovery that brought him great joy. It will be remembered that his watch kept London time, and that he refused to put its hands forward. All the clocks in all the countries he had passed through, he said, were wrong. Now on this day, although he had put its hands neither forward nor backward, the watch marked the same time as the clock on the ship. He wished that Fix were there so that he could show him that his watch kept the right time after all.

"The silly fool was talking to me about the sun and the moon and the movement of the earth. If we listened to what all those men said, we should have a very funny sort of time. I was certain that one day the sun would come to agree with my watch!"

But there was something that Passepartout did not know. If his watch was marked from one to twenty-four hours (as some clocks are) he would not have been so happy about it. For in that case, instead of pointing to nine o'clock (as it did), it would have been pointing to twenty-one o'clock.

But if Fix had been able to explain this, Passepartout would not have been able to understand the explanation, or to accept it. In any case, if the police-detective had shown himself at that moment, it is probable that Passepartout would have had something to say to him on quite a different subject.

Where *was* Fix at that moment?

He was, in fact, on the *General Grant*.

When he reached Yokohama, he left Mr Fogg, whom he expected to meet again late in the day, and went at once to the British consul. There he found the warrant. It had been following him all the way from Bombay, and was already forty days old. It had been sent on from Hong Kong by the *Carnatic*, on which steamer he was himself believed to be. We may imagine the disappointment of Fix. The warrant had now become useless. Mr Fogg was now outside the reach of the English law.

"Very well!" Fix said to himself, after his first moment of anger. "The warrant is of no use here, but it will be of use in England. It looks as if this bank robber is going back to his country after all. Very well. I will follow him there. As for the money he stole, I hope there will still be some left. But with the cost of the journey, the presents he gives, the elephant he bought, and the rest, my man must have left more than five thousand pounds on the way. However, the Bank of England is rich."

Having made up his mind, he went at once to the *General Grant*. He was there when Mr Fogg and Aouda came on board. To his great surprise he saw Passepartout in his strange clothes and long nose. So he hid himself in his cabin. The number of passengers was so great that he hoped that his enemy would not see him. But today, in the front part of the ship, he suddenly met him.

Without saying a word, Passepartout jumped at Fix and, to the great joy of some Americans (who at once began to bet on the result of the fight), attacked him, striking him again and again.

When he had finished knocking him down, Passepartout felt much better and calmer. Fix got up and said coldly:

"Have you finished?"

"Yes, for the moment."

"Then come and have a talk with me."

"Have a talk with you! I ——"

"Yes, for the sake of your master."

Passepartout seemed to be overcome by the calm way in which Fix spoke, and followed him. They both sat down.

"You have given me a beating. Very well. Now listen to me. Up to the present I have been your master's enemy, but now I am on his side."

"Oh, at last, then, you believe him to be an honest man."

"No, I don't," answered Fix coldly, "I believe him to be a thief. Be quiet, and let me speak. So long as Fogg was on British ground I tried to hold him back while I was waiting for the warrant to arrest him. I did all that I could do to stop him. I sent the priests from Bombay to Calcutta; I made you drunk at Hong Kong; I separated you from him and made him lose the boat to Yokohama."

Passepartout listened, ready to fly at Fix again.

"Now," Fix went on, "Mr Fogg seems to be going back to England. Very well, I will follow him. But from now on, I will help him in his journey as much as I have tried to stop his journey. You see that my plan has changed. It is changed because it is to my interest to change it. I will add that your interest is the same as mine, for it is only in England that you will come to know whether you are serving an honest man or a thief."

Passepartout listened carefully to what Fix was saying, and felt sure that Fix was not going to play any more tricks.

"Are we friends?" asked Fix.

"No, not friends," answered Passepartout, "but we can help each other. But if you start playing any more tricks I will certainly break your neck!"

"All right," said the police-detective calmly.

13

A Quarrel in San Francisco

Eleven days after that the *General Grant* reached San Francisco. Mr Fogg was neither a day too late nor a day too early.

As soon as he got on shore he asked at what time the first train left for New York. The answer was: "At six o'clock this evening." Mr Fogg had, then, a whole day to spend in San Francisco. He called a carriage and they drove to the International Hotel.

After a good meal Mr Fogg, with Aouda, went to the British consul to show his passport and have it signed.

When they came out, Passepartout said:

"As we are going to travel through a wild part of the country where we might be attacked by Indians, would it not be wise to buy a few revolvers with which to protect ourselves?"

Mr Fogg answered that he thought that was not at all necessary, but Passepartout could go and buy some if he liked.

Phileas Fogg had hardly walked a hundred steps when he met

Fix. The police-detective seemed to be most surprised at this meeting.

"What a strange thing!" he said, "that we should meet by chance like this. To think that we both travelled on the *General Grant* without once seeing each other."

Anyhow, Fix was most pleased, he said, to meet again the gentleman to whom he owed so much. He was forced to go back to Europe on business, and it would be very pleasant if they could travel together.

Mr Fogg answered that it would be an honour for him. Fix who did not wish to lose sight of the man he was following, asked to be allowed to join him in the visit round the town.

So Aouda, Phileas Fogg and Fix walked through the streets. They saw crowds of excited people. Some were shouting, "Long live Kamerfield!" and others, "Mandiboy for ever!"

"This seems to be an election," said Fix to Mr Fogg, and added, "Perhaps it would be well to keep away from the crowd, or we might get hurt." Fix was now very anxious that nothing should happen to Mr Fogg. It was now to his interest to take care of him and protect him from harm, so that he could arrest him when they reached England.

"You are right," answered Phileas Fogg and he, Aouda and Fix went and stood at the top of some stone steps where they could see what was going on below.

What election was this? Phileas Fogg had no idea.

At this moment the crowd became very excited. The people rushed here and there shouting loudly. Fix was just going to ask somebody what all this meant, but before he could do so a general fight broke out. Stones and bottles were thrown; and sticks were used freely. A crowd of people came shouting up to the steps at the top of which Mr Fogg and his companions were standing.

"I think we had better go away," said Fix.

"They cannot hurt us; we are English ——" Mr Fogg began to say, but before he could finish, another crowd came up to them from behind. They were caught between the two. No escape was possible. Phileas Fogg and Fix, in protecting the young lady, were knocked this way and that. Mr Fogg, as calm as ever, was going to defend himself, when a big fellow with red hair raised his hand and struck a violent blow. Mr Fogg would have suffered severely if Fix had not received the blow instead.

"Fool of an American!" said Mr Fogg, looking calmly at his attacker.

"Fool of an Englishman!" answered the other.

"We shall meet again!"

"When you like. Your name?"

"Phileas Fogg. Your name?"

"Stamp W. Proctor."

At that moment the crowd moved on. Fix was knocked down but he got up again at once. His clothes were torn but he was not seriously hurt.

"Thank you," said Mr Fogg to the police-detective, as soon as they were out of the crowd.

"Do not thank me," answered Fix, "but come with me."

"Where?"

"To a shop where we can buy some new clothes."

It was in fact quite necessary to do this, for, as a result of the fight, their clothes had been torn to pieces. An hour later, wearing new hats and coats, they went back to the hotel.

Passepartout was waiting for his master. He was holding the revolvers that he had been buying. He looked anxious when he saw Fix in company with his master. But when Aouda explained to him what had happened, he felt happy again. It was clear that Fix was keeping his promise and was no longer an enemy.

When dinner was over Mr Fogg sent for a carriage to take the travellers and their luggage to the station. Mr Fogg said to Fix:

"You have not seen any more of this Stamp W. Proctor?"

"No," answered Fix.

"I shall come back from England to find him again," said Phileas Fogg. "It is not right that an Englishman should be treated as he treated me."

At a quarter to six, the travellers reached the station and

found the train ready to start.

The railway on which they were to travel runs from San Francisco to New York, a distance of 3,786 miles. As the journey took seven days, Mr Fogg had every reason to suppose that he would reach New York just in time for him to take the steamer that left for Liverpool on December 11th.

The travellers left Oakland station at six o'clock. It was already dark, and the sky was covered with black clouds. The train did not move with any great speed; perhaps twenty miles an hour, counting stops.

Nobody talked much. Passepartout found himself sitting next to the police-detective, but he did not speak to him. There was a certain coldness between the two — and this was only natural.

An hour later it began to snow.

At eight o'clock the travellers were told that it was time to get the beds ready for the night, and in a few minutes their carriage was changed into a bedroom. There was only one thing to do and that was to go to bed and sleep. And while the travellers were sleeping the train steamed across California. In six hours' time the train reached the important city of Sacramento. From San Francisco the country had been fairly flat, but now the train began to climb the mountains of Nevada. At seven o'clock the train passed through Cisco.

An hour later the beds were packed away, and the travellers looked out of the windows and were able to see the mountainous country through which they were passing. There were few or no bridges. The train ran up and round the sides of the mountains or passed along the bottom of the narrow valleys.

At Reno the travellers stopped for twenty minutes during which time they were able to have breakfast. Then they took their places again in their carriage and watched the country through which they were passing. At times they saw large numbers of buffaloes. By crossing the railway line in their thousands, these animals often force the trains to stop and wait until they have passed. In fact this is what soon happened. About twelve o'clock the train came to a place where ten or twelve thousand buffaloes were walking slowly across the line. It was impossible to move them or go through this solid body of animals. The only thing to do was to wait until the line was clear.

The travellers watched this strange sight with interest. Phileas Fogg stayed in his seat and waited patiently. Passepartout, however, was terribly angry, and very much wanted to start shooting them with his revolvers.

"What a terrible country!" he cried. "A country in which they allow animals like these to get in the way of trains! I wonder whether Mr Fogg expected this sort of thing when he planned his journey. And here is the engine-driver afraid of running his engine through them."

The engine-driver, of course, was wise enough to do nothing of the sort. It would have been useless. He could no doubt have crushed the first buffaloes, but the engine would soon have been stopped and certainly thrown off the line.

It was three hours before the last of the animals crossed the railway, and it was dark before the train could go on again.

By December 7th they had gone far. On this day they stopped for a quarter of an hour at Green River station. It had been snowing and raining during the night, but as the snow had half melted it gave no trouble. The bad weather, however, worried Passepartout.

"What a foolish idea it was to go travelling during the winter," he said to himself. "If my master had waited for better weather, he would have had better chances of winning his bet."

But while Passepartout was worrying about the weather, Aouda began to be frightened about something much more serious. Looking out of the window she saw among the group of travellers Stamp W. Proctor, the man who had behaved so roughly in the election fight at San Francisco. It was only by accident that he happened to be on the same train, but there he was. "He must be prevented," she thought, "from meeting Mr Fogg."

When the train was on its way again, and Mr Fogg happened

to be asleep, Aouda told Fix and Passepartout whom she had seen.

"Proctor on this train!" cried Fix. "Well, have no fears; it is my business rather than Mr Fogg's. After all, I am the one who suffered most."

"And I shall have something to say to him, too," added Passepartout.

"Mr Fix," said Aouda, "you may be certain that Mr Fogg will let nobody take his place in this matter. He said he would even come back to America to meet this man again. If he sees Mr Proctor, we cannot prevent them from fighting, and this might have sad results. They must not meet each other."

"You are right," said Fix. "A fight might spoil everything. Whether he won or lost, Mr Fogg's chances of success would be in danger."

"And that would suit the gentlemen of the Reform Club," added Passepartout. "In four days we shall be in New York! Well, if during those four days Mr Fogg does not leave his carriage, we may hope that he will not meet this man."

At this moment Mr Fogg woke up, and the talk came to an end. Later, without being heard by his master or Aouda, Passepartout said to the police-detective:

"Would you really fight instead of him?"

"I will do everything to bring him back alive to Europe," answered Fix.

Was there any way to keep Mr Fogg in the carriage so as to prevent him from meeting this Proctor? It should not be difficult, for Mr Fogg did not care to move about. In any case, the detective thought of a good way and, a few minutes later, said to him:

"Time passes very slowly in the train."

"Yes," answered the other, "but it passes all the same."

"On the boat," said Fix, "you used to play cards."

"Yes," answered Phileas Fogg, "but here it would be difficult. I have neither cards nor people to play with."

"Oh, as for the cards, we can easily buy them. They are sold on all American trains. As for people to play with, if by chance the lady plays —— "

"Oh, yes," answered the lady. "I know the game that Mr Fogg likes playing."

"So do I," said Fix. "In fact I know the game rather well. So the three of us —— "

"Very well; if you would care to do so," answered Phileas Fogg, who was very pleased to have the chance of playing again.

Passepartout was sent to get the cards, and soon came back with everything that was necessary for the game. A table covered with a cloth was brought, and they started playing. Aouda really played very well, and Mr Fogg told her so. As for Fix, he was a first-class player.

"Now," thought Passepartout, "everything is safe. He will not move from the table."

14

Full Speed!

At eleven o'clock in the morning the train reached one of the highest points on its journey through the Rocky Mountains. Two hundred miles farther they would be at last on those immensely wide stretches of flat country that lie between the mountains and the Atlantic coast. A few hours more and they would have passed the difficult and dangerous part of their journey through the mountains.

After a good midday meal the travellers began playing again. Before long, however, the train moved more and more slowly and then stopped.

Passepartout put his head out of the window but saw nothing that might explain the stop. No station was to be seen.

For a moment Aouda and Fix were afraid that Mr Fogg would want to get down from the train. But he only turned to Passepartout and said:

"Go and see what's the matter."

Passepartout jumped out. Thirty or forty travellers had got out, and among them was Stamp W. Proctor.

The train had stopped in front of a red signal. The engine-driver and the train officials had got down and were with a man who had been sent to stop the train. They were talking very seriously about something. Some of the travellers came up and joined in the talk, among others Mr Stamp W. Proctor, with his rough loud voice.

Passepartout heard the man say:

"No, you can't possibly get past! The bridge at Medicine Bow is in need of repair, and will certainly not support the weight of the train."

The bridge of which they were talking was one that hung across a deep river about a mile farther on. What the man said was quite true. The bridge was unsafe.

Passepartout, not daring to go and inform his master, stayed and listened.

"Well," said Mr Proctor, "we are not going to stand here for ever in the snow!"

"Sir," answered the railway official, "we have sent a telegram to Omaha asking them to send a train to meet us at Medicine Bow, but it can hardly get here in less than six hours."

"Six hours!" cried Passepartout.

"Yes," said the official. "In any case it will take us that time to walk as far as the station."

"Walk?" cried all the travellers.

"But how far away is the station, then?" asked someone.

"Twelve miles from the other side of the river."

"A twelve mile walk in the snow!" cried Stamp W. Proctor. Then he broke out into violent language, calling the railway company and its official all the bad names he could think of. Passepartout, who was equally angry, felt like joining him. Here was something against which it was no use fighting. All the bank notes of his master were useless to overcome the difficulty.

The disappointment of the passengers was great. Not only would they be late but they would have to walk fifteen miles through the snow. The noise of their complaints would certainly have been noticed by Phileas Fogg if that gentleman had not been so interested in his game.

Passepartout then saw that he would have to tell his master what had happened, and he turned to go to the carriage, when the engineer, a true American, named Foster, raised his voice and said:

"Gentlemen, there is one way of getting across."

"Across the bridge?" asked somebody.

"Yes, across the bridge."

"With our train?" asked Proctor.

"With our train."

Passepartout stopped, and listened to what was being said.

"But the bridge is unsafe!"

"That doesn't matter," said the engineer. "I believe that by making the train go at full speed, there will be a good chance of getting over."

"Well, what a mad idea!" thought Passepartout.

But quite a number of the travellers very much liked the idea, particularly Stamp W. Proctor.

"Quite reasonable and quite natural!" he cried.

"Why," he went on, "there are engineers who are now making plans for trains going at full speed to cross rivers without any bridge at all!"

In the end all the travellers agreed to the idea.

"We have fifty chances of crossing," said one.

"Sixty," said another.

"Eighty, ninety chances out of a hundred!"

Passepartout was too surprised to speak or even to think. He was ready for any plan to cross the river, but this one seemed to him to be rather too "American".

"Besides," he thought, "there is a much simpler way, and these people have not even thought of it."

"Sir," he said to one of the travellers, "the plan seems to me a little dangerous, but —— "

"Eighty chances out of a hundred!" answered the traveller, turning his back to him.

"I know," said Passepartout, turning to somebody else, "but I have been thinking —— "

"There is nothing more to be said," answered the man. "The engineer says we can get across, and that is an end of the matter."

"Yes, I am sure we can get across," said Passepartout, "but would it not be less dangerous —— "

"What's that! Dangerous?" cried Proctor. "Don't you understand? At full speed!"

"Yes, I know; I understand," said Passepartout — again nobody allowing him to finish what he wanted to say. "But don't you think it would be more natural —— "

"What? What's that? What's he talking about?" everybody shouted.

"Are you afraid?" asked Proctor.

"Afraid? I, afraid?" cried Passepartout. "I'll show these Americans whether a Frenchman is afraid!"

"Take your seats! Take your seats!" shouted the railway official.

"All right! All right!" shouted Passepartout to him. "But I can't help thinking that it would be more natural for us to walk over the bridge first, and then let the train follow!"

But nobody heard this wise advice, and in any case nobody would have agreed to the idea.

The travellers all went back to their seats, and Passepartout went back to his, without saying anything of what had happened. The card-players were sitting there thinking only of their game.

The engine-driver made the train go back nearly a mile, in the same way as a jumper steps back before he makes his jump. Then he made it go forward again quicker and quicker; soon the train was running at a terrible speed. It seemed to be at the rate of a hundred miles an hour. It flew over the bridge! Nobody even saw the bridge. The train simply jumped from one side of the river to the other, and the driver could not stop it until it was five miles on the other side of the station.

But the train had hardly passed over when the bridge, broken to pieces, fell with a crash into the water below.

That evening the train reached the highest point of its journey, 8,091 feet above the sea. It now had only to go down until it reached the Atlantic. The travellers had now come 1,382 miles from San Francisco in three days and nights. In four days and four nights more they should be at New York.

The next day the travellers were playing cards as usual. None of them complained of the length of the journey. Fix had begun by winning a few pounds, and was now beginning to lose them again. Mr Fogg now held very good cards; he was just going to play a certain black card when a voice was heard behind him saying:

"Don't play that; play that red card instead."

Mr Fogg, Aouda and Fix looked up. Stamp W. Proctor was standing there.

"Oh, it's you, is it, Mr Englishman!" cried he. "You are the one who wants to play the black card."

"Yes, and I play it," answered Phileas Fogg, as he did so.

"Well, I want you to play the other." And the man bent forward to take hold of it, adding, "You don't know how to play this game."

"Perhaps there is another game that I know better," said Phileas Fogg, getting up from his seat.

"Well, you can try," said Proctor with an ugly smile on his face.

Aouda looked very frightened. She took hold of Mr Fogg's arm, but he gently pushed her from him. Passepartout was ready to throw himself on the American, but Fix stood up and, going to Proctor, said:

"The quarrel is between you and me. You were not only disrespectful towards me, but you even struck me."

"Mr Fix," said Mr Fogg, "I beg your pardon, but this is my business alone. This man will answer to me for his behaviour."

"When and where you like," answered the American.

Aouda tried to hold Mr Fogg back, but unsuccessfully. The detective tried to take the quarrel upon himself. Passepartout wanted to throw the American out of the window, but a sign from his master stopped him. Phileas Fogg went out of the carriage and the American followed him.

"Sir," said Mr Fogg to his enemy, "after our meeting in San Francisco I made up my mind to come back to America to find you as soon as I had finished the business that calls me to England."

"Really!"

"Will you meet me in six months' time?"

"Why not in six years' time?"

"I said six months," answered Mr Fogg.

"You want to escape from me!" cried Stamp W. Proctor. "You will fight me now or never."

"Very well," answered Mr Fogg. "You are going to New York?"

"No."

"Chicago?"

"No."

"Omaha?"

"That's no business of yours. Do you know Plum Creek?"

"No," answered Mr Fogg.

"It's the next station. The train will be there in an hour's time. It will wait there for ten minutes. That will give us time enough to fight."

"Agreed," said Mr Fogg. "I will stop at Plum Creek."

"And I believe you will stay there!" said the American, with an ugly laugh.

"Who knows, sir?" answered Mr Fogg, who went back to his seat.

Then he said a few words to Aouda to calm her anxiety.

"People who talk loudly and boast are not to be feared," he said. Then he took Fix on one side and asked him to serve as his supporter. Fix could not refuse, and Phileas Fogg picked up his cards and went on with his game.

At eleven o'clock the train reached Plum Creek station. Mr Fogg got up, and followed by Fix, went out of the car. Passepartout went with him, carrying a pair of revolvers.

At this moment the door opened and Mr Proctor came out, too, followed by a friend. But just as the two enemies were going to step down, the chief of the train ran up, saying:

"Nobody is to get down here, gentlemen."

"Why not?" asked Proctor.

"We are twenty minutes late, and the train does not stop."

"But I have to fight this gentleman."

"I am sorry," said the official, "but we are starting at once. There is the bell ringing."

As he said this the train started again.

"I am really very sorry, gentlemen," said the train official. "I should like to have helped you. But, after all, as you have no time to fight here, is there any reason why you should not fight on the train?"

"Perhaps that would not suit this gentleman," said Proctor in an unpleasant voice.

"It will suit me perfectly," answered Phileas Fogg.

"We are certainly in America!" thought Passepartout. "And the chief of the train is a perfect gentleman!" Saying this, he followed his master.

The two men, their two friends, and the train official passed through the carriages until they reached the end of the train. In the last carriage there were only about ten people. The official asked them whether they would be good enough to give up the carriage for a few minutes to two gentlemen who wished to fight.

Why, of course! The people were only too happy to be of any service to the two gentlemen, and at once went out and stood in the passages.

The carriage was fifty feet long, and very suitable for what was to be done. The two men could walk towards each other between the seats and shoot at each other at their ease. The fight was very easy to arrange. Mr Fogg and Mr Proctor, each carrying two revolvers, went into the car. Each revolver had six shots in it. The two supporters would shut the door and stay outside. A signal would be given and shooting would begin. Then after two minutes the door would be opened and what was left of the two gentlemen would be carried out. Nothing could be simpler.

15

An Attack by Indians

But before the signal could be given, wild cries and shots were heard. The shots certainly did not come from the car in which the two gentlemen were shut. Bang! Bang! Bang! The shots came from the outside — all along the train. Cries of terror were heard from one end of the train to the other.

Mr Proctor and Mr Fogg with their revolvers in hand, jumped out of their car and rushed forward, where shouts and shots were growing louder at every moment.

They saw that the train had been attacked by Sioux Indians.

This was not the first time that these Indians had attacked a train, and more than once before they had been successful. According to their usual habit, a hundred of them had jumped on the steps of the moving train and had climbed up onto the roof of the cars.

These Sioux had guns. From these guns came the shots that had been heard. The passengers answered with their revolvers. First of all the Indians had jumped on the engine and had knocked down the engine-driver and his man. One of the Indians tried to stop the train but not knowing how to do so had opened the steam pipe instead of shutting it. The result was that the train was flying along at full speed.

At the same time the Sioux had broken their way into the cars and were fighting with the passengers. The cries and shots went on without stopping.

The passengers, however, defended themselves bravely. Among these was Aouda. With a revolver in her hand she fired through the broken windows at any Indian that came in sight. Twenty or more of the Indians fell dead or wounded on the railway line, and the wheels crushed any who fell between the cars.

Several of the passengers, badly wounded, were lying on the seats.

The end must come before long. Fighting had been going on for ten minutes, and the Sioux must get the best of it if the train did not stop. Fort Kearney station was only two miles away. At this station were soldiers; but if the train passed this point the Sioux would certainly become masters of the train.

The chief of the train was fighting by the side of Mr Fogg when a shot struck him and he fell. He cried out:

"We are all lost if the train does not stop in five minutes."

"The train will stop," said Phileas Fogg who was going to rush out of the car.

"Stay where you are, sir," cried Passepartout to him. "This is my business."

Phileas Fogg had no time to stop the brave fellow who, opening one of the doors without being seen by the Indians, managed to climb under one of the cars.

While the fight went on, and with shots flying in the air over his head, Passepartout crawled under the carriage and made his way forward under the cars, holding on here and there, and jumping from one place to another until he got to the front part of the train. There, hanging on by one hand, he managed to undo the heavy iron fastenings that joined the cars to the engine. He could hardly have finished doing this if a sudden shock had not helped him. The train, now separated from the engine, began to run more and more slowly while the engine flew forwards with still greater speed.

The train ran along for a few minutes but soon came to a stop less than three hundred feet from the station. Hearing the shots, the soldiers ran up towards the train. The Indians did not wait for them and, before the train stopped, all ran off.

But when the passengers were counted, it was found that three did not answer to their names, and among them was the Frenchman· whose bravery had saved the train. What had happened to them? Had they been killed in the fight? Were they prisoners of the Indians? Nobody yet knew.

Many of the passengers were wounded but none of them seriously. One of the wounded was Mr Proctor, who had fought bravely. He was taken to the station with the others, where they received every care.

Aouda was safe. Phileas Fogg was safe, too, although he had been fighting all the time. Fix was slightly wounded in the arm. But Passepartout was not to be found; and tears ran down the face of the young lady who owed her life to him now for the second time.

Mr Fogg stood there without speaking. He had to make a serious decision. If his servant had been taken prisoner, it was his duty to try to rescue him.

"I shall find him, alive or dead," he said simply to Aouda.

"Oh, Mr Fogg," cried Aouda, taking his hands in hers and covering them with tears.

"I shall find him alive," added Mr Fogg, "if we lose no time."

By this decision Phileas Fogg would lose everything. If he were only one day late he would fail to catch the boat at New York. His bet was lost. But with the thought, "It is my duty," he had made up his mind.

The captain and a hundred soldiers were there. It was their business to defend the station against any attack by Indians.

"Sir," said Mr Fogg to the captain. "Three people have disappeared."

"Dead?" asked the captain.

"Dead or prisoners," answered Phileas Fogg. "That is what we must find out. Do you mean to follow the Indians and catch them?"

"That is a serious matter, sir," answered the captain. "These Indians may run two or three hundred miles away. I cannot leave this station that is under my protection."

"Sir," said Phileas Fogg, "it is a question of the lives of three men."

"Quite true, but can I put the lives of fifty men in danger to save three?"

"I don't know whether you can, but that is what you ought to do."

"Sir," answered the captain. "I will allow nobody here to teach me my duty."

"Very well, then," said Phileas Fogg coldly. "I will go alone."

"You!" cried Fix, who had come up to the two men. "You would go after these Indians alone?"

"Do you think that I am going to leave that brave fellow to die, who saved the lives of everybody here? I shall go."

"Well, sir," cried the captain. "You will not go alone. No, you have a brave heart. Now! Who offers to join this gentleman? Thirty men are wanted!" he said, turning to his soldiers.

The whole company stepped forward. The captain only had to choose among them. Thirty were named, and an officer put at their head.

"Thank you, captain!" said Mr Fogg.

"You will allow me to come with you?" asked Fix.

"You may do as you like," Fogg answered. "But if you wish to be of real service to me, you will stay by the side of this lady, and take care of her."

The detective's face turned white. What! Separate himself from the man that he was following so patiently? Let him go off alone into the wild country? Fix looked at Mr Fogg for a moment and then in spite of his feeling he looked away from Fogg's calm, serious face.

"I will stay," he said.

A few minutes later Mr Fogg gave the young woman his bag,

telling her to take great care of it, shook hands with her, and went off with the officer and his little company of men.

Before leaving, he said to the soldiers, "There is a thousand pounds for you if we save the prisoners."

It was then a few minutes after midday.

Aouda had gone into the waiting room of the station, and there, alone, she thought of Phileas Fogg, this kind and brave man. He had given up his fortune and was now putting his life into danger. In her eyes he was a great and worthy man.

The detective Fix did not think at all that way, and could not hide his feelings. He walked up and down outside the station, reproaching himself for his foolishness in letting him leave.

"I was a fool!" he thought. "Fogg had come to know who I was! He has gone, and will not come back. Where shall I find him again? How could I have been tempted to let him go; I, who have in my pocket the warrant for his arrest?"

Those were the thoughts of Fix while the hours slowly passed. He did not know what to do. Sometimes he felt like telling Aouda everything. Sometimes he felt like going off across the snow to catch this Mr Fogg. It would not be impossible to find him again. He could still follow the footprints of the soldiers in the snow. Before long the falling snow would cover them again.

Then Fix felt like giving everything up as lost and going straight back to England. If he decided to do so, there was nothing to prevent him, for at two o'clock, while the snow was falling heavily, the noise of an engine was heard coming from the east. But no train was yet expected from the east. The help for which they had asked could not come so quickly, and the train from Omaha to San Francisco would only reach them the next day. They soon came to know what it was.

It was the engine of their train. It had rushed on for many miles, then the fire had gone lower for want of coal. There was no more steam, and an hour later the engine, running more and more slowly, had come to a stop twenty miles on the other side of Kearney station.

Neither the engine-driver nor his helper had been killed; and after some time had passed, they had come to their senses. When they found that they were alone and that the train was no longer there, they guessed what had happened. How the engine had become separated from the train is what they did not know.

They could go on to Omaha; that was the wisest thing to do. They could go back towards the train; that was dangerous. The Indians might still be on the train. The driver soon made up his mind what to do. They must go back. Coal and wood were put on the fire; the water soon became hot again, and before long there was enough steam to make the engine move, and at two o'clock it reached Kearney station.

The passengers were all happy when they saw the engine once more at the head of the train. They could now go on again with their journey.

When the engine came into the station, Aouda left the station and went up to the chief of the train.

"You are leaving?" she asked.

"At once."

"But the prisoners, our unfortunate fellow-travellers?"

"I am sorry we cannot wait for them. We are already three hours late."

"And when does the next train come from San Francisco?"

"Tomorrow evening."

"Tomorrow evening? But that will be too late. You must wait."

"That is impossible," answered the official. "If you want to come with us, you must get on the train at once."

"I shall not come," answered the lady.

Fix had heard this talk. A few moments before that, when there was no way of leaving, he had wanted to get away. Now that the train was there, and he had only to take his place in the carriage, he no longer wanted to leave. The fight in his mind began all over again. He was overcome by his sense of failure.

During this time the passengers had taken their places on the train, among them the wounded Mr Proctor — whose condition was serious. The noise of steam was heard. The bell rang, the train moved out of the station and was soon lost to sight in the snow.

The detective had stayed behind.

Some hours passed. The weather was bad and it was very cold. Fix was sitting on a seat in the station; he might have been asleep. Aouda, in spite of the snow-storm, would go out of the room, walk to the end of the station buildings, look out and listen. But she saw and heard nothing.

Evening came. The little company of soldiers did not come back. Where were they? Had they been able to catch up with the Indians? Had there been a fight? The captain was very anxious, but tried not to show his anxiety.

Night came. The snow was no longer falling so heavily, but it got colder and colder. No sound was to be heard.

During the whole of the night Aouda, with a heavy heart and fearing the worst, walked about outside. In her imagination she could see a thousand dangers.

Fix did not move, but he, too, was awake. At one moment a man came up to him and said something. But Fix simply answered, "No."

In this way the night passed. The sun rose in a grey sky. Phileas Fogg and the soldiers had gone towards the south, but nothing was to be seen to the south except the snow.

The captain, now very anxious, did not know what to do. Should he send a second company to the help of the first? At last he called one of his officers and gave him orders to send out a few men towards the south — when suddenly shots were heard. Was it a signal? The soldiers rushed out and half a mile away they saw the others coming back.

Mr Fogg was at the head of the company, and by his side was Passepartout and the two other travellers rescued from the Sioux.

There had been a battle ten miles to the south of Kearney. A little before the soldiers reached them Passepartout and his two companions had started fighting against those who had taken them prisoners. The Frenchman had already knocked three of them over when his master and the soldiers rushed up to their help.

At the station they were all welcomed with shouts of joy, and Phileas Fogg gave the soldiers the reward that he had promised them. Passepartout said more than once:

"I have certainly cost my master a lot of money!"

Fix looked at Mr Fogg without saying a word. It would be difficult to say what were the thoughts that passed through his mind. Aouda went up to Phileas Fogg, took his hands and pressed them, without being able to say a word.

As soon as he reached the station Passepartout looked round to find the train. He was expecting to see it there ready to leave for Omaha, and hoped that they would be able to make up for the time lost.

"Where's the train?" he cried.

"Gone," answered Fix.

"And the next train?" asked Phileas Fogg.

"Will not come before this evening."

"Ah!" was all that the gentleman answered.

16

A Sledge with Sails

Phileas Fogg then found himself twenty hours late on his journey. Passepartout reproached himself with being the cause.

At that moment Fix walked up to Mr Fogg and said:

"Are you really in a hurry to get on?"

"I really am," answered Phileas Fogg.

"You really want to get to New York by the 11th before nine o'clock in the evening, when the boat leaves for Liverpool?"

"I do."

"And if your journey had not been stopped by the attack on the train, you would have reached New York on the morning of the 11th?"

"I should. I should have been in time by twelve hours."

"Very well. You are twenty hours late. Between twelve and twenty there is a difference of eight. You must regain them. Do you wish to do so?"

"On foot?"

"No, on a sledge," answered Fix. "On a sledge with sails. A man has offered us the use of one."

This was the man who had spoken to Fix during the night and whose offer Fix refused.

Phileas Fogg did not answer, but Fix having pointed to the man who was walking up and down in front of the station, Mr Fogg went up to him. A few moments later Phileas Fogg and this American, named Mudge, went inside a hut not far away.

There Mr Fogg examined this strange sledge. It was built of wood, and was large enough to hold five or six people. It had a high mast, which carried a large sail. At the back was a sort of rudder by which the sledge could be made to go in any direction. It was a sort of ship, but instead of being made to travel through the water it sailed along on the ice or snow. During the winter, when trains are stopped by the snow, these sledges could go with great speed from one station to another.

In a few moments an arrangement was made with the owner of the sledge. The wind was right. It blew from the west with great force. The snow was hard and Mudge promised to take Mr Fogg to Omaha in a few hours. From Omaha there are many trains running on more than one railway towards Chicago and New York. In this way it would be quite possible to make up for lost time, and there was no reason why the plan should not be tried.

As Aouda might suffer from the cold, Mr Fogg thought of leaving her with Passepartout at Kearney station, and the Frenchman promised to bring her to Europe a little later by train and boat.

But Aouda refused to be separated from Mr Fogg, and Passepartout was very happy at her decision. He had no wish to leave his master alone with Fix.

It would be difficult to say what Fix was thinking of all this. Had he changed his ideas about Mr Fogg when he saw this gentleman come back, or did he think of him still as a cunning fellow who thought that after his journey round the world he would be safe in England? Perhaps he now thought better of Mr Fogg. But in any case he decided to do his duty, and was as anxious as anybody to get back to England as soon as possible.

At eight o'clock the sledge was ready to start. The travellers took their places on it, well covered up and protected against the cold. The sail was raised, and with the wind behind it, the sledge flew forward at a speed of forty miles an hour.

The distance between Kearney and Omaha in a straight line was not more than two hundred miles. If the wind did not drop it would be possible to do this distance in five hours. If there were no accident the travellers should be in Omaha by one o'clock.

It was a cold journey. The travellers pressed against each other for warmth. The cold, made greater by the speed, made it impossible for them to speak. The sledge slid across the snow as lightly as a boat on the water. When the wind blew strongly it seemed that the sledge would be lifted up in the air. Mudge kept the sledge going in the right direction.

"If nothing breaks, we shall get there," said Mudge.

It was to the interest of Mudge to get there in time, for Mr Fogg, as usual, had offered him a big reward.

The country over which they passed was as flat as the sea. It looked like an immense frozen lake.

There was nothing in the way and there were only two things to be afraid of: that something might break or that the wind might fall.

But the wind did not fall. It blew stronger than ever. It made the mast bend, but the sledge was so solidly built that there was no danger of anything breaking.

Passepartout now had a face as red as the setting sun. He

began to hope again. Instead of getting to New York in the morning, they would get there in the evening, but they had a good chance of catching the boat. He was so happy that he was almost ready to shake hands with Fix and call him his friend. He did not forget that it was Fix himself who had thought of the sledge, which was the only way of getting to Omaha in time. And yet he did not trust Fix; he felt that the detective was still ready to play some trick.

One thing that Passepartout would never forget was the way in which Mr Fogg had gone back to rescue him from the Indians. To do that he had put his life and fortune in danger. No, he would never forget that.

At twelve o'clock Mudge saw that he had crossed the River Platte. He said nothing, but he was already sure that he would reach Omaha station twenty miles farther.

It took them just an hour. The sledge stopped, and Mudge pointed to a few hundred houses with snow-covered roofs.

"We are there," he said.

Yes, they were really there. They had reached a station from which trains ran many times a day to the east.

Passepartout and Fix jumped off the sledge, glad to stretch their legs again after five hours without movement. They helped Mr Fogg and the young woman to get down. Phileas Fogg gave the promised reward to Mudge, and Passepartout shook his hand as if he were an old friend, and they all hurried to the station.

A train was ready to start, and Mr Fogg and his companions only just had time to jump into the carriage. They had seen nothing of Omaha, but Passepartout thought that was nothing to be sorry about.

At great speed the train passed through the country separating them from Chicago. The next day, the 10th, at four o'clock in the evening they reached this famous city, already rebuilt after the terrible fire that had destroyed it a few years before.

Nine hundred miles separate Chicago from New York. There

were plenty of trains. Mr Fogg and his companions had only to get down from their train and to step into another. The engine started off at full speed as if it knew that Mr Fogg had no time to lose. The train flew across the country, through Indiana, Ohio, Pennsylvania and New Jersey. They sometimes passed through towns that had not yet any houses built in them.

At last they saw the Hudson River, and on December 11th, at a quarter past eleven in the evening, the train came to a stop at the station close to the quay of the Steamship Company.

17

Mr Fogg Tries to Find a Ship

Three-quarters of an hour earlier, the steamship *China* had left for Liverpool!

In leaving New York the *China* seemed to have taken with it Mr Fogg's last hope.

No other boat would suit his plan. The French boat would leave only on the 14th, two days later. The German boat was not going to Liverpool or London; it would call at a French harbour — and Mr Fogg would not be able to get from there to London in time.

One steamer, it is true, would be leaving the next day, but it was no use thinking of that, for it was a slow boat, using sails rather than steam.

Passepartout was completely overcome by disappointment. Three-quarters of an hour too late! It was his fault, he thought. Instead of helping his master he was the cause of making him late. When he thought of all the things that had happened during the journey from London, when he thought of all the money spent uselessly, and of the losing of the bet, he was filled with self-reproach.

He received no reproaches, however, from Mr Fogg, who said simply:

"Well, we will think about the matter tomorrow."

The group of travellers went to a hotel. Mr Fogg was the only one who slept.

The next day was the 12th of December. From the 12th, at seven in the morning, to the 21st, at eight forty-five in the evening, there were left nine days thirteen hours and forty-five minutes. If, then, Phileas Fogg had started the night before in the *China*, one of the fastest ships of the Steamship Company, he would have got to Liverpool, and then to London, in time.

Phileas Fogg left the hotel alone, having told his servant to wait for him, and to let Aouda know that she must be ready to start at any moment.

Mr Fogg went to the harbour and looked among the ships for any which were getting ready to start. He found more than one, for in this immense harbour there is not a day when a hundred boats do not leave for every part of the world. But most of these were sailing boats, and they would not suit Phileas Fogg.

At last he noticed a fine-looking steamer. The clouds of smoke that she was sending out of her chimney showed that she was getting ready to start.

Phileas Fogg called a boat, got into it, and in a few moments found himself by the side of the *Henrietta*, an iron steamer with her upper parts of wood.

The captain of the *Henrietta* was on board. Phileas Fogg went up and asked for the captain, who came at once.

He was fifty years old, a rough-looking, disagreeable man. His large eyes, red hair and big body did not give him a pleasant appearance.

"The captain?" asked Mr Fogg.

"I am he."

"I am Phileas Fogg, of London."

"And I am Andrew Speedy, of Cardiff."

"You are going to start?"

"In an hour."

"You are going to leave for —— ?"

"Bordeaux."

"You have passengers?"

"No passengers. Never have passengers. I prefer goods. Goods don't get in the way, and they don't talk."

"Yours is a quick ship?"

"Between eleven and twelve miles an hour. The *Henrietta* is well known for its speed."

"Are you willing to take me to Liverpool, myself and three persons?"

"To Liverpool. You might as well say China."

"I said Liverpool."

"No!"

"No?"

"No. I am starting for Bordeaux, and I shall go to Bordeaux."

"It doesn't matter what price?"

"It doesn't matter what price."

The captain spoke in a voice that showed it was useless to reason with him.

"But the owners of the *Henrietta*," replied Phileas Fogg.

"The owners of the *Henrietta* are myself," replied the captain. "The ship belongs to me."

"I will hire it from you."

"No."

"I will buy it from you."

"No."

Phileas Fogg kept calm. But the position was serious. At New York it was not as at Hong Kong, nor with the captain of the *Henrietta* as with the captain of the *Tankadere*. Until now the gentleman's money had always been able to get over difficulties. This time the money failed.

They could not, of course, cross the Atlantic by air; that would be too dangerous, and besides, impossible, so a way must be found of crossing the Atlantic in a ship.

Phileas Fogg, however, seemed to have an idea, for he said to the captain:

"Well, will you take me to Bordeaux?"

"No, even if you were to pay me forty pounds."

"I will pay you four hundred pounds."

"For each person?"

"For each person."

"And there are four of you?"

"Four."

Captain Speedy did not know what to think. Sixteen hundred pounds to be earned without changing any plans; it was well worth the trouble of forgetting his dislike of passengers. Besides, passengers at four hundred pounds each are no longer passengers, but valuable goods.

"I leave at nine o'clock," said Captain Speedy simply, "and you and your people will be here?"

"At nine o'clock we will be on board," simply replied Mr Fogg.

It was half past eight. To land from the *Henrietta*, get into a carriage, go back to the hotel, and take from there Aouda, Passepartout, and even Mr Fix, to whom he kindly offered a passage — all this was done by the gentleman with the calmness which never left him even when he was in the greatest trouble.

At the moment that the *Henrietta* was ready to sail, all four were on board. An hour later the steamer passed out of the Hudson River. During the day she steamed along the shore of Long Island, and then went out into the open sea.

At twelve o'clock the next day, the 13th of December, a man went up to the bridge and began giving orders to the officers, telling them exactly in what direction the ship must go.

It would certainly be supposed that this man was Captain Speedy. Not at all. It was Phileas Fogg!

As for Captain Speedy, he was locked up in his cabin and was roaring with anger — and this was not surprising.

What had happened was very simple. Phileas Fogg wanted to go to Liverpool; the captain would not take him there. Then Phileas Fogg had agreed to pay to go to Bordeaux, and during the thirty hours that he had been on board he had spent money so cleverly and wisely that the officers and men — who very much disliked the captain — belonged to him. And that is why Phileas Fogg, and not Captain Speedy, was master of the ship, why the captain was shut up in his cabin, and why, lastly, the *Henrietta* was making her way not towards Bordeaux but towards Liverpool. Seeing Mr Fogg sail the ship, it was very clear that he had once been a sailor. Now, what the end of this adventure was going to be, nobody could tell.

But in any case Aouda felt very anxious about it, although she said nothing. Fix was so surprised that he said nothing. Passepartout found the thing simply splendid!

"Between eleven and twelve miles an hour," Captain Speedy had said, and this seemed true.

If, then, the sea did not get too rough, if the wind did not blow from the east, if there was no accident to the ship, the *Henrietta* in the nine days, counting from the 12th of December to the 21st, would cross the three thousand miles separating New York from Liverpool.

During the first days they went along in particularly good conditions. The wind was not too rough, and blew from the right direction. The sails were raised, and with them the *Henrietta* sailed as fast as any of the regular steamers.

Passepartout was very, very happy, but he preferred not to think about what might happen later. The officers and men had never seen a merrier or more lively fellow. He made friends with the sailors, calling them by all sorts of loving names, and giving them all sorts of good things to drink. He thought that they worked the ship like gentlemen and brave men. He made others feel as happy as himself. He had forgotten the past, with its troubles and dangers. He thought only of the end, which was so near, and sometimes became terribly impatient.

Fix, it must be said, did not understand anything at all. The taking of the *Henrietta*, the buying of her officers and men, and Fogg behaving as a regular sailor — this was too much for him. He did not know what to think. But, after all, a man who began by stealing fifty-five thousand pounds could finish by stealing a ship. Of course, he believed that Fogg was not going to Liverpool at all, but into some part of the world where the robber would find a safe place to live in. This supposition seemed most reasonable, and Fix began to be sorry for having come into the business at all.

As for Captain Speedy, he kept on roaring in his room, and Passepartout, whose duty it was to give him his food, did it only with the greatest care, in spite of his great strength.

18

Mr Fogg Buys the Henrietta

On the 13th they passed close by the island of Newfoundland. This is a dangerous part of the Atlantic. Here, particularly during the winter, there is much fog. There were signs that the weather was going to change. During the night it had grown colder, and at the same time the wind began to blow from the south-east.

This was a misfortune. Mr Fogg, so as not to be driven out of the right direction, had to take down the sails and to use more steam. But the ship went more slowly because of the condition of the sea. Long waves broke against the ship and made her roll violently. The wind got stronger and stronger until it blew a regular storm. For two days Passepartout was very frightened. But Phileas Fogg was a daring sailor, who knew how to keep the ship going against the sea. The *Henrietta*, whenever she could rise with the waves, passed over them, but the water often poured across the ship from end to end.

Still, the wind did not get too severe. It was not one of those storms in which the wind blows at the rate of ninety miles an hour. But unfortunately it blew all the time from the south-east, so that the sails could not be used. And yet, as we shall see, it would have been very useful if they could have come to the help of the steam.

The 16th of December was the seventy-fifth day that had passed since their start from London. The *Henrietta* was not seriously late, half of the crossing was almost over, and the worst part of it had been passed. In summer, success would have been certain. In winter, they had to trust to the weather. Passepartout said nothing. In his heart he had hopes. "If we cannot depend on the wind," he thought, "we can at least depend on the steam."

Now, on this day, the chief engineer came up from below, met Mr Fogg, and had a very serious talk with him. Without knowing why, Passepartout felt a sort of fear. He would have given one of his ears to have heard with the other what was said. But he could catch a few words, these among others, said by his master:

"You are certain of what you say?"

"I am certain, sir," answered the other. "Do not forget that, since we left, all our fires have been burning, and although we had enough coal to go in the usual way from New York to Bordeaux, we have not enough to go as we are now going, from New York to Liverpool."

"I will think over the matter," replied Mr Fogg.

Passepartout understood. He was terribly frightened.

The coal was just coming to an end.

"Ah! if my master can get over that difficulty," he said to himself, "he will certainly be a wonderful man!"

He could not help telling Fix the state of things.

"Then," answered the detective, "you believe that we are going to Liverpool?"

"I really do."

"Fool," answered Fix, as he turned away.

And now what was Phileas Fogg going to do? It was difficult to guess. But it appeared that that calm gentleman had decided on a plan, for that evening he sent for the engineer and said to him:

"Keep your fires going, and keep going the same direction

until there's no more coal left."

About twelve o'clock Phileas Fogg sent for Passepartout and ordered him to go and bring Captain Speedy. Passepartout did not like having to do that, and he went down below, saying to himself: "It is quite certain that I shall find him perfectly mad!"

A few minutes later a madman came up on deck shouting and roaring. It was Captain Speedy. He looked as if he were going to burst.

"Where are we?" were the first words he said in his terrible anger.

"Where are we?" he roared again.

"Seven hundred and seventy miles from Liverpool," answered Mr Fogg, with great calmness.

"Thief!" cried Andrew Speedy.

"I have sent for you, sir —— "

"Robber!"

"Sir," continued Phileas Fogg, "I have sent for you to ask you to sell me your ship."

"No!"

"I am going to burn her."

"To burn my ship!"

"At least the wooden part, for we have no more coal."

"Burn my ship!" cried Captain Speedy, who was so angry that he could hardly speak. "A ship that is worth ten thousand pounds!"

"Here are twelve thousand pounds," said Phileas Fogg, holding out the money to him.

The result of this offer was to make Andrew Speedy forget his anger, his imprisonment and all his reasons for complaint against Mr Fogg. His ship was twenty years old. It might be quite a good business for him.

"And I can keep what is left of the ship after you have burnt the wooden parts?" asked he, in a strangely soft voice.

"Yes, all the iron part will still be yours."

"I agree."

And Andrew Speedy took the money and pushed it into his pocket.

During this talk the face of Passepartout had turned white. Twelve thousand pounds spent, and yet Fogg was going to give back to the seller all the iron part of the ship, that is, almost the whole value of the ship.

When Andrew Speedy had put the money in his pocket, Mr Fogg said to him:

"Sir, don't let all this surprise you. I shall lose twenty thousand pounds if I am not in London on the twenty-first of December at a quarter to nine in the evening. Now I was not able to catch the regular steamer from New York, and as you would not take me to Liverpool ——"

"And I did well to say no," cried Andrew Speedy, "because by doing so I have put at least ten thousand pounds into my pocket."

"Now this ship belongs to me?" asked Fogg.

"Certainly, from top to bottom; that is to say, all the wood, understand."

"Very well. Cut away the wood and put it on the fires."

One can easily imagine how much of this wood was needed to get enough steam.

The next day, the 19th of December, they burnt much more of the wooden part of the ship. The men worked very hard, and Passepartout worked harder than anybody else.

The next day, the 20th, almost all the woodwork of the ship above water was burnt. But on this day the coast of Ireland came into sight.

At ten o'clock in the evening the ship was passing Queenstown. Phileas Fogg had only twenty-four hours to reach London! Now this was the time the *Henrietta* needed to reach Liverpool. And there was little or no more steam.

"Sir," then said Captain Speedy, who had come to be interested in Mr Fogg's plan, "I am really very sorry for you. Everything is against you. We are so far only off Queenstown."

"Ah!" said Mr Fogg, "that is Queenstown, the place where we see the light?"

"Yes."

"Can we go into the harbour?"

Not for three hours. Only at high water."

"Let us wait," Phileas Fogg replied calmly, without letting it be seen on his face that, by a last plan, he was going to try to succeed!

Queenstown is where the steamers coming from America leave the bags of letters. These letters are carried to Dublin by fast trains always ready to start. From Dublin they are sent to Liverpool by very fast ships, and in this way they get to Liverpool twelve hours before the fastest ships of the steamship companies.

These twelve hours Phileas Fogg meant to use. Instead of reaching Liverpool by the *Henrietta* in the evening of the next day, he would be there by twelve o'clock, and so he would have time enough to get to London before a quarter to nine in the evening.

Towards one o'clock in the morning the *Henrietta* came into Queenstown harbour at high water, and Phileas Fogg, having received a most friendly shake of the hand from Captain Speedy, gave him what was left of his ship, still worth half of what he had sold it for!

The passengers landed at once. They jumped into the train at Queenstown at half past one in the morning, reached Dublin just when it was beginning to get light, and at once went on board one of those famous steamers which, instead of rising with the waves, always pass right through them.

At twenty minutes to twelve, the 21st of December, Phileas Fogg landed at Liverpool. He was now only six hours from London.

But at that moment Fix went up to him, put his hand on his shoulder saying:

"Your name, I believe, is Phileas Fogg."

"Yes."

"In the name of the Queen, I arrest you."

19

Mr Fogg Is in Prison

Phileas Fogg was in prison. They had shut him up at the police station at Liverpool and he was to spend the night there. The next day he would be taken to London.

At the moment of the arrest Passepartout tried to throw himself on the detective, but he was held back by the policemen. Aouda, terrified at what she saw, could understand nothing. Passepartout explained the matter to her. Mr Fogg, this honest and brave gentleman, to whom she owed her life was arrested as a thief. The lady cried out that such an accusation was impossible, but she soon saw that she could do nothing to save the one who had saved her.

As for Fix, he had arrested Mr Fogg because it was his duty to arrest him, whether he was guilty or not. The law would decide the matter.

Then a thought came to Passepartout, the terrible thought that it was certainly he himself who was the cause of this misfortune. After all, why had he hidden the matter from Mr Fogg? When Fix had informed him, Passepartout, who he was and what he was going to do, why had he not told his master? If his master had known of what he was accused he could certainly have proved to Fix that he was not guilty. In any case Mr Fogg would not have helped Fix to follow him and even bear the cost of his travelling! In thinking of his foolishness in saying nothing, the poor fellow was overcome by self-reproach. Tears ran from his eyes. It was painful to see him.

In spite of the cold, Aouda and he had stayed on the quay. Neither of them would leave the place. They wanted to see Mr Fogg once again.

Mr Fogg had lost everything at the very moment when he was

going to win. He had reached Liverpool at twenty minutes to twelve on December 21st. He had until a quarter to nine to get to the Reform Club, that is to say, nine hours and fifteen minutes — and the journey to London was one of six hours.

Anybody who could have seen Mr Fogg in the police station would have found him sitting quietly, on a wooden seat, without anger and perfectly calm. There he waited. For what was he waiting? Had he any hope of success?

Mr Fogg had carefully put on a table his watch, and he looked at it as time went on. Not a word escaped from him. In any case his position was terrible, and for anyone who could read his thoughts his position was this:

As an honest man, Phileas Fogg had lost everything.

As a dishonest man, he was taken.

Had he any idea of escaping from his prison? Did he think of getting out? Perhaps so, for at a certain moment he walked round the room examining it. But the door was solidly locked, and the window could not be opened. He sat down again and took out his pocketbook. To the line that had written on it the words:

December 21st, Saturday, Liverpool,

he added:

80th day. 11.40 in the morning

and he waited.

One o'clock struck. Mr Fogg noticed that his watch was two minutes faster than the clock.

Two o'clock. If he could get into a train now it would not be too late to get to the Reform Club by twenty minutes to nine.

At thirty-two minutes past two, a noise was heard outside, a noise of opening doors. He could hear the voice of Passepartout and the voice of Fix.

The door opened, and he saw Aouda, Passepartout and Fix, who ran towards him.

Fix was out of breath, his hair was in disorder. He could hardly speak.

"Sir . . . sir . . . forgive me . . . a mistake . . . somebody who looked like you . . . The thief . . . arrested three days ago. You . . . are . . . free!"

Phileas Fogg was free. He went up to the detective. He looked him full in the face, and then making the only quick movement that he had ever made in his life, knocked the unfortunate detective down.

Fix, lying on the ground, said nothing. He had got his reward. Mr Fogg, Aouda, Passepartout went out. They threw themselves into a carriage and in a few moments reached Liverpool station.

Phileas Fogg asked whether there was a train leaving for London.

It was twenty minutes to three. The train had left thirty-five minutes earlier.

Phileas Fogg then ordered a special train.

There were several engines ready for such a journey but arrangements could not be made at once, and the special train could not leave before three o'clock.

At three o'clock, Phileas Fogg, after having said something to the engine-driver about a certain reward for speed, was on his way to London, in the company of the young lady and his faithful servant.

It was necessary to do the distance between Liverpool and London in five hours. This is quite possible when the line is free from end to end. But several times the train was forced to stop, and when the train came into the station at London, all clocks showed the time to be ten minutes to nine.

Phileas Fogg, having completed his journey round the world, was five minutes late.

He had lost.

The next day the people who lived in Savile Row would have been very surprised if they had been told that Mr Fogg had come home. The doors and windows were all shut, and the house looked like an empty one.

When he left the station, Phileas Fogg had given orders to Passepartout to buy what was necessary for meals and then went home. He had received with his usual calmness the blow that had struck him. All was lost, and by the fault of the police-detective. After having successfully done what he had hoped to do, in spite of all difficulties and dangers, and having still had time to do good on the way, to fail at the moment of reaching the end of his journey, to fail because of something most unexpected and of no fault of his own; it was terrible. Hardly anything was left of the large sum that he had taken away with him. All the money he now had in the world was the twenty thousand pounds lying in his bank, and this he owed to his friends of the Reform Club. Having spent so much on his journey, the winning of the bet would not have made him any richer — and it is probable that he had not wished to become any richer, but the losing of the bet left him without any money at all. But he had made up his mind. He knew what he was going to do.

It was arranged that a room in the house in Savile Row should be got ready for Aouda. She was in a most unhappy state. From certain words that she had heard Mr Fogg say, she guessed that he was thinking of putting an end to his life. For this reason Passepartout watched his master closely.

The night passed. Mr Fogg had gone to bed, but had he slept? Aouda could not sleep for a moment. Passepartout, like a faithful dog had watched at his master's door all night.

The next morning Mr Fogg called him and told him to see to Aouda's breakfast. He asked to be excused from seeing her, as all his time was given to putting his business in order. He would not come down, but in the evening he would ask to speak to Aouda for a few moments.

Passepartout having received these orders had only to carry them out. He looked at his master and could not decide to leave the room. His heart was heavy. He accused himself more than ever for this sad ending to the adventure. Yes, if he had warned his master about Fix's plans, Mr Fogg would certainly not have brought the detective with him to Liverpool, and then ——

"Master! Mr Fogg!" he cried. "Reproach me. It is by my fault that ——"

"I reproach nobody," answered Phileas Fogg in the calmest of voices. "Go."

Passepartout went to Aouda and gave the message.

"My good fellow, do not leave your master alone — not for a moment. You say that he wants to see me this evening?"

"Yes. I think that he wants to make arrangements for your protection in England."

"Then we'll wait," said she.

During the day it was as if nobody were living in the house. Phileas Fogg did not go to the club.

Why should he go to the club? His old companions there were not expecting him. As he had not appeared at the club the evening before, at a quarter to nine, his bet was lost.

At half past seven in the evening Mr Fogg asked whether Aouda would receive him, and a few moments later they were alone in the room.

For five minutes he said nothing. Then, raising his eyes, he said:

"Will you forgive me for bringing you to England? When I had the idea of bringing you away from the country that had become so dangerous for you, I was rich, and expected to offer you a part of my fortune. Your life would have been happy and free. Now I am poor."

"I know that, Mr Fogg," answered the young lady, "and I will ask you this — will you forgive me for having followed you, and — who knows — for having been one of the causes of your failure?"

"You could not have stayed in India, and for your safety it was necessary for you to get away."

"Then, Mr Fogg," she went on, "it was not enough for you to save me from a terrible death, you thought yourself forced to take care of my future."

"That is so, but I was unfortunate. In any case my plan is to give you the little that I have left."

"But you, Mr Fogg, what shall you do?"

"I am in need of nothing for myself."

"But do you know what you are going to do?"

"I shall do what it is right for me to do."

"In any case, a man such as you cannot ever be in real want. Your friends ——"

"I have no friends."

"Then I am sorry for you, Mr Fogg, for it is sad to be without friends. It is said that misfortune can be borne when there are two to bear it."

"So it is said."

"Mr Fogg," she then said, getting up and holding out her hand to him, "will you have me as your friend? Will you have me as your wife?"

At these words Mr Fogg stood up. For a moment he shut his eyes. When he opened them again he said:

"I love you. Yes, I love you and am yours!"

He at once called Passepartout. He came. He saw his master and Aouda holding hands. He understood, and his face filled with joy.

Mr Fogg asked him whether it was too late for him to go to call on the Reverend Samuel Wilson at once to make arrangements for a marriage.

Passepartout smiled. "It is never too late," he said.

It was only five minutes past eight.

"It will be for tomorrow, Monday," he added.

"For tomorrow, Monday?" asked Mr Fogg, looking at Aouda.

"For tomorrow, Monday!" she answered.

Passepartout ran out of the house.

20

A Mistake in the Day

On the Saturday evening the five gentlemen had met at the Reform Club at eight o'clock.

When the clock pointed to five and twenty minutes past eight, Andrew Stuart got up and said:

"Gentlemen, in twenty minutes' time Mr Fogg must be here or he will lose his bet."

"At what time did the last train from Liverpool reach London?" asked Thomas Flanagan.

"At twenty-three minutes past seven. The next train gets to London at ten minutes past midnight."

"Well, gentlemen," said Andrew Stuart, "if Phileas Fogg had come by the seven twenty-three he would already be here. We may safely say that we have won the bet."

"We must wait," said one of the others. "You know that Mr Fogg is a man of very exact habits. He never gets anywhere too late nor too early. If he came into this room at the last moment I should not be surprised."

"As for me," said Andrew Stuart, "even if I saw him I shouldn't believe it. He has certainly lost. The *China*, the only steamer by which he could have come from America in time, reached Liverpool yesterday. Here is the list of people who were on it, and the name of Phileas Fogg is not among them. I imagine that he has hardly yet reached America. He will be at least twenty days late."

"That is certain," said another. Tomorrow we shall only have to go to the bank and receive the money."

The clock pointed to twenty minutes to nine.

"Five minutes more," said Andrew Stuart.

The five friends looked at each other. Their hearts were

perhaps beating a little faster than usual, for even among those who were used to betting, this bet was for a very large sum of money.

"I would not give up my four thousand pounds," said Andrew Stuart, "if I were offered three thousand nine hundred and ninety-nine pounds for it!"

At that moment the clock pointed to sixteen minutes to nine.

Only one minute more and the bet would be won.

They began to count the seconds.

At the fortieth second, nothing happened. At the fiftieth second nothing happened.

At the fifty-fifth second, a noise like thunder was heard outside the room, a noise of shouting.

At the fifty-seventh second the door of the room opened, and before the hand of the clock reached the sixtieth second, Phileas Fogg appeared followed by a large crowd of people who had forced their way into the building. He said in his usual calm voice:

"Here I am, gentlemen."

Yes! Phileas Fogg himself.

It will be remembered that at five minutes past eight — about twenty-five hours after the travellers had arrived in London — Passepartout had been sent by his master to the Reverend Samuel Wilson to make arrangements for a certain marriage to take place the next day.

He left the house full of joy and happiness.

The Reverend Samuel Wilson had not yet come home. Of course Passepartout waited. He waited at least twenty minutes.

It was thirty-five minutes past eight when he left the house. But in what a state! His hair in disorder and without any hat, running and running as nobody had ever run before, knocking people over as he ran.

In three minutes he was back at the house in Savile Row, and he fell breathless into Mr Fogg's room.

He could not speak.

"What's the matter?" asked Mr Fogg.

"Master! . . . marriage . . . impossible."

"Impossible?"

"Impossible . . . for tomorrow."

"Why?"

"Because tomorrow . . . is Sunday!"

"Monday," answered Mr Fogg.

"No . . . today . . . Saturday."

"Saturday? Impossible!"

"Yes, yes, yes," cried Passepartout. "You have made a mistake of one day. We reached London twenty-four hours early. But we have only ten minutes!"

Passepartout took his master and pulled him out of the room.

Phileas Fogg, carried off without having the time to think, left the house, jumped into a carriage, promised a hundred pounds to the driver, and after having run over two dogs and knocked against five other carriages, reached the Reform Club.

The clock pointed to a quarter to nine when he came into the room where the members were waiting.

Phileas Fogg had done this journey round the world in eighty days.

Phileas Fogg had won the bet of twenty thousand pounds.

And now, how could such a careful man have made such a mistake? How was it that he believed it to be Saturday evening, December 21st, when it was only Friday, December 20th, seventy-nine days only since he had left?

This is the reason for the mistake. It is very simple.

Phileas Fogg had made his journey by going towards the east. As he travelled towards the sun the days got shorter by four minutes every time he crossed one of the 360 degrees by which the earth is measured. In other words, while he saw the sun pass over him eighty times, the members of the Reform Club saw it pass only seventy-nine times. That is why on that day, which was Saturday and not Sunday, the members were waiting for him. If he had travelled towards the west, he would have lost a day on the way and would have reached London one day late.

Phileas Fogg had won the twenty thousand pounds. But as he had spent about nineteen thousand on the way, he made little profit. And of the thousand pounds that was left he gave half to the faithful Passepartout and the other half to the unfortunate Fix, against whom he bore no anger.

That same evening Mr Fogg, as calm and cold as usual, said to Aouda:

"Are you still willing to marry me?"

"Mr Fogg," she answered, "it is I who ought to ask you that question. You were poor; now you are rich."

"Excuse me," he said, "but this fortune belongs to you. If you had not had the idea of this marriage, my servant would not have gone to the Reverend Samuel Wilson; I should not have known about the mistake in the day, and ——"

"Dear Mr Fogg," said the lady.

"Dear Aouda," answered Phileas Fogg.

Of course the marriage took place forty-eight hours later, and Passepartout in a wonderful state of joy, had the place of honour by the lady's side at the church.

And what had Phileas Fogg gained by this journey?

"Nothing," you may say.

Very well, nothing! Except a beautiful and loving wife who — strange as it may seem — made him the happiest of men.

And was that not worth a journey round the world?

Questions

Questions on factual details

Chapter 1

1   Give three examples of Phileas Fogg's regular habits.
2   Why did Phileas Fogg decide to go round the world?
3   How did he plan to prove to his friends that he had been round the world?

Chapter 2

4   Why couldn't the detective keep Mr Fogg in Suez?
5   Why did Passepartout say: "The sun may be wrong, but not my watch"?
6   How did Passepartout make Mr Fix even more suspicious about Mr Fogg?

Chapter 3

7   What did Passepartout do that made the priests in the temple so angry?
8   When the train stopped, why did Mr Fogg say he expected it?

Chapter 4

9   What was the Indian custom of *suttee*?
10 Who was Aouda?

Chapter 5

11 How did Passepartout save Aouda?
12 Give two examples of Phileas Fogg's kindness in this chapter.

Chapter 6

13 Why did Phileas Fogg and Passepartout think that the police had arrested them?

14 What was the real reason for their arrest?
15 Why did Mr Fix worry that Phileas Fogg was spending so much money?

Chapter 7
16 Why did Passepartout think Mr Fix was following Mr Fogg?
17 When the *Rangoon* did not go fast enough, what did Passepartout and Mr Fogg do?

Chapter 8
18 Why did Mr Fix want to keep Fogg and Passepartout in Hong Kong?
19 Why was Mr Fix pleased that Passepartout was so drunk?

Chapter 9
20 What did Mr Fogg feel when he learnt that the *Carnatic* had sailed without him?
21 Why did Mr Fogg go to Shanghai instead of Yokohama?

Chapter 10
22 Why did Mr Fix think it was important that Passepartout should not meet his master again?
23 Mr Fogg and the pilot of the *Tankadere*, John Bunsby, felt differently about the approaching storm. Why?
24 Why did Mr Fogg tell Mr Bunsby to fire a cannon?

Chapter 11
25 How did Passepartout catch the *Carnatic* when Mr Fogg and Aouda missed it?
26 Why did he eat so much on the ship?
27 Why did Mr Batulcar let Passepartout join his company of acrobats?
28 Why did Passepartout cause the human pyramid to collapse?

Chapter 12

29 How were Aouda's feelings towards Phileas Fogg changing?

30 Why was Mr Fix disappointed when he finally got the warrant to arrest Phileas Fogg?

31 Why did Mr Fix change his plan and decide to help Mr Fogg reach England?

Chapter 13

32 Why did Mr Fogg think that the American crowds in San Francisco would not hurt them?

33 How did Mr Fix prevent Phileas Fogg from meeting Stamp W. Proctor on the train?

Chapter 14

34 Passepartout thought the plan to cross the broken bridge was "rather too 'American' ". What did he mean?

35 At Plum Creek, why did Passepartout think the chief of the train was a "perfect gentleman"?

Chapter 15

36 When the Indians attacked the train, why was it important to stop the train near Fort Kearney station?

37 How did Passepartout save the train from disaster?

38 What was Phileas Fogg's "duty"?

Chapter 16

39 How did Mr Fix help Mr Fogg continue his journey?

40 How did the sledge move along?

41 Why was it important to reach Omaha?

Chapter 17

42 Why did Phileas Fogg not leave on the steamer which was going the next day?

43   Why did Mr Fogg lock up Captain Speedy of the *Henrietta*?

Chapter 18
44   What did Mr Fogg do when the *Henrietta* had no more coal?
45   How did they go from Queenstown in Ireland to Liverpool?

Chapter 19
46   Why did Passepartout feel so bad when Mr Fogg was arrested?
47   Why was Mr Fogg set free?
48   Why didn't he go straight to his club?

Chapter 20
49   Explain how Phileas Fogg had made a mistake with the day.
50   How did Aouda help Phileas Fogg to win the fortune?

Questions on the whole novel

1   At the beginning of *Round the World in Eighty Days*, Phileas Fogg writes a plan for how long each part of the journey will take. Make notes on how long each part actually takes, and then give reasons for the differences.
2   Phileas Fogg is "certainly English, a fine-looking English gentleman". Give examples of Fogg's behaviour and actions which show what Jules Verne meant by "English".
3   What are the differences in character between Phileas Fogg and Passepartout?
4   Describe the different kinds of transport that Phileas Fogg and Passepartout used to travel round the world.
5   Write an account of the actual cost of each part of Phileas Fogg's journey.
6   Draw a map of the world and show the route which Phileas Fogg followed.
7   What are the reasons that make Mr Fix think that Phileas Fogg is the bank robber? Is there any moment in the story when you agree with him?

8   Why do you think Phileas Fogg never believed Mr Fix was following him?

9   Write Aouda's diary from the time she wakes up (in Allahabad) until the moment she asks Phileas Fogg to marry her in London.

10   Describe in Passepartout's own words his adventures in Yokohama until he finds Phileas Fogg. Start: "And so I arrived in this strange Land of the Rising Sun". . .

11   Describe Mr Stamp W. Proctor's character.

12   Imagine you are Captain Speedy. Describe what happens to you from when you first meet Phileas Fogg in New York, until you reach Queenstown.

13   Why is Passepartout such a funny person?

14   Why do you think Phileas Fogg always manages to stay calm in the face of difficulties?

15   Several of the names of people in the book show something about their characters. Give three examples and explain what they show.

16   What kind of place was America in the 1870s, according to Jules Verne?

17   *Round the World in Eighty Days* was written in 1873, when the British Empire was at its height. How does the story show this?

18   Which part of the journey do you think is most exciting and why?

19   After you have read *Round the World in Eighty Days*, do you want to travel more or less? Why?

20   Describe the route that you would take if you were going to travel round the world.

Glossary

acrobat a person skilled in balancing on ropes or wires, walking on their hands, etc.; **acrobatic** = of, or like, an acrobat

armchair a comfortable chair with supports for the arms

arrest to seize by the power of the law; **an arrest** = the act of arresting

bail money left with a court of law so that a prisoner can be set free until he or she is tried

bet an agreement to risk money on the result of a future event, by which the person who guesses wrongly gives the money to the other person; **a bet** = a sum of money risked in this way

bow to bend the upper part of the body forward, as a way of showing respect

buffalo a large wild cowlike animal, with a very large head and shoulders covered in hair

cabin a room on a ship usually used for sleeping

canal an artificial waterway dug in the ground

cannon a large powerful gun

consul a person appointed by a government to protect and help its citizens in a foreign city

crawl to move slowly with the body close to the ground, or on hands and knees

crew all the people working on a ship

cunning clever in deceiving; cleverness in deceiving

deck a floor built across a ship over all or part of its length

exceptional unusual, especially of unusually high quality

fog very thick mist

harbour an area of water by a coast which is sheltered from rougher waters so that ships are safe inside it

mast a long upright pole of wood for carrying sails on a ship

merchant a person who buys and sells goods in large amounts

overcome to make helpless; defeat

passport a small official book which proves who a person is and allows them to leave their country and enter foreign countries

pyramid a solid figure with a flat, usually square, base and straight flat three-angled sides that slope upwards to meet at a point

quay a place where boats can stop to load and unload, usually built of
   stone and usually forming part of a harbour
reproach blame; **to reproach** = to blame (someone), usually sadly
Reverend a title for a Christian priest
revolver a small gun
rudder a blade at the back of a ship that is swung from side to side to
   control the direction in which it moves
sake; for the sake of for the purpose of; in order to help
sightsee to make a tour of interesting places
sir a respectful way of addressing a man
Sir a title given to a man by the king or queen
sledge a vehicle made for carrying people or goods over snow,
   having two long metal blades
steam to travel by steam; **at full steam** = at the fastest speed
steamer a large ship driven by steam power
telegram a message sent by using radio signals or electrical signals
   along a wire
tightrope a tightly stretched rope or wire, high above the ground,
   on which skilled people walk and do tricks
warrant a written order signed by an official of the law